Advance praise for
Marcy Dermansky and *Bad Marie*

"Reading Marcy Dermansky's *Bad Marie* is like spending a rainy afternoon in a smaller, older movie theater watching a charming French movie with a woman (or a man) you've just met on the street and already like far too much. It's sinful in all the right ways, delicate, seditious, and deliciously evil."

— Frederick Barthelme, author of *Waveland*

"By positing a character who's indulged in all of the deadly sins, Dermansky challenges the reader to finally and forever denounce her character Marie. The fact that this reader can't is testament to the book's power and smarts. A naughty pleasure, a philosophical romp, heady hedonism: What could be better?"

— Antonya Nelson, author of *Nothing Right*

"Marcy Dermansky is one of the most demanding novelists of our generation—she leaves her readers little time for friends, food, or sleep. *Bad Marie* is impossible to turn away from. It is as empathic as it is disturbing, as delicate as it is savage. Sly, honest, and extraordinary, this gem of a book should come with a warning: You'll have to remind yourself to breathe."

— Tish Cohen, author of *The Truth About Delilah Blue*

"If you've ever wondered what it would be like to say just what you think to people who annoy you, to walk away from your life, to enjoy the comfort of strangers, then I suspect you will find *Bad Marie* irresistible. In swift, vivid prose Marcy Dermansky has created a wonderful portrait of a woman who lives right at the edge of acceptable behavior. I couldn't wait to see what Marie would do next, and I couldn't stop myself from cheering her on."

— Margot Livesey, author of *The House on Fortune Street* and *Eva Moves the Furniture*

"What I don't know about the inner lives of women could fill a book—but not this book, which has a title character that is bad in all the right ways and all the better for it. Marcy Dermansky's *Bad Marie* is all about the tricksy margins of human experience, stolen moments and the people who steal them."

— Ben Greenman, author of *What He's Poised to Do* and *Please Step Back*

"Marcy Dermansky makes it easy to love Marie, a husband-stealing, baby-snatching, underachieving ex-con. The author sends us rocketing along on a brilliant, bumpy ride across the ever-changing landscape formed by the simple loves, the staggering losses and the bad choices that are Marie's life. Fast-paced and unsentimental, *Bad Marie* blazes with life."

— Barb Johnson, author of *More of This World or Maybe Another*

"*Bad Marie* unfolds in precise, gripping measure. But as the story keeps taking a turn for the worse, ratcheting up the tension, it is buoyed by the lovely relationship at its heart. The unlikely bond between Marie and Caitlin brings our heroine comfort and love in a world determined to deny her both."

— Mark Sarvas, author of *Harry, Revised*

"Marcy Dermansky's *Bad Marie* is so very very bad that I enjoyed every word. A tour de force in mounting suspense as its witless narrator and the baby she's stolen careen from one all-too-probable disaster to the next. Delicious."

— Terese Svoboda, author of *Cannibal* and *Pirate Talk or Mermelade*

"I didn't want to finish this book any time soon, didn't want to emerge from its dark and wondrous world. My God, what a writer—absolutely unpredictable, wild with intellect, spilling with charm and sadness and humanity. Marie, the main character here, is literary gold, worthy of Flaubert."

— Mary Robison, author of *Why Did I Ever*

"Compelling, dark, and like a traffic accident that you try to look away from, only to find your gaze returning with odd fascination. . . . This well-written book gives readers a voyeuristic, insiders' glimpse into the lives of not only twins, but teenagers . . . [C]omically and darkly entertaining."

— *Denver Rocky Mountain News*

"[A] startlingly beautiful love story about two very unlikely identical twins. It's a joy—no, a thrill—to read. . . . This is easily the most detailed, disturbing, and lovable oddball romance you'll ever read. Dermansky is a writer through and through." — Frederick Barthelme, author of *Waveland*

"Entertaining. . . . Balanced by an overarching fable-like quality to this moving and well-written story of two girls learning to accept who they are." — *Publishers Weekly*

"Raw, extraordinary. . . . A dark, heartbreaking tale about adolescents trying to survive." — *Huntsville Times* (AL)

"Marcy Dermansky's *Twins* is spectacular, weird, extraordinarily real, and funny in ways they don't have names for. The perils of contemporary adolescence—from pill-popping to not eating to bad tattoos—are chronicled with an immediacy so intense it's almost alarming. Dermansky inhabits her characters with a savage, hysterical eloquence. Her novel grabs your heart from the first sentence, and breaks it by the end."

— Jerry Stahl, author of *I, Fatty*

Also by Marcy Dermansky

Twins

BAD MARIE

A NOVEL

MARCY DERMANSKY

HARPER 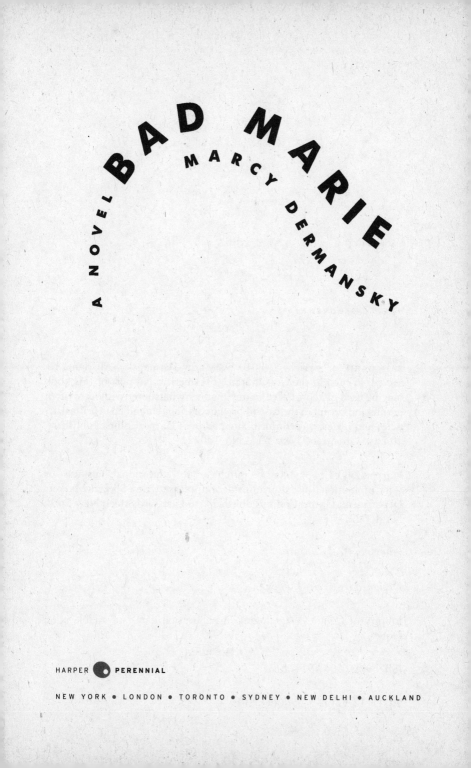 PERENNIAL

NEW YORK • LONDON • TORONTO • SYDNEY • NEW DELHI • AUCKLAND

HARPER ● PERENNIAL

HarperCollins books may be purchased for educational, business, or
sales promotional use. For information, please write: Special Markets
Department, HarperCollins Publishers, 10 East 53rd Street, New York,
NY 10022.

FIRST EDITION

Designed by Aline C. Pace

Library of Congress Cataloging-in-Publication data is available upon
request.

ISBN 978-0-06-191471-3

10 11 12 13 14   OV/RRD   10 9 8 7 6 5 4

For Jürgen

Sometimes, Marie got a little drunk at work.

She took care of Caitlin, the precocious two-and-a-half-year-old daughter of her friend Ellen Kendall. It was a full-time job. Marie got paid in cash and was given a room in the basement.

She never drank in the daytime. Only at night. Marie didn't see the harm: a little whiskey, a little chocolate. Marie liked to watch bad movies on TV while Caitlin slept. She liked wandering over to the fully stocked refrigerator and helping herself to whatever she wanted to eat. Marie constantly marveled over the food: French cheeses, leftover steak, fresh-squeezed orange juice, raspberries imported from Portugal. It had only been three weeks since Marie's thirtieth birthday, the day that she had gotten out of jail.

The situation would have been humiliating had Marie any ambition in life. Fortunately, Marie was not in any way ambitious. Changing diapers and making lunch, taking Caitlin out for walks to the neighborhood park—these were things that Marie could do. Marie liked living in Manhattan. She liked listening to the lilted banter of the other nannies from the neighborhood, mainly black women from the West Indies. Marie even liked the educational TV she watched with Caitlin. *Sesame Street* was just Marie's speed. She often napped during Caitlin's afternoon naptimes.

Marie, who hadn't felt much of any emotion since her boyfriend had killed himself in prison nearly six years ago, found herself crazy in love with a two-and-a-half-year-old girl. It unnerved Marie, how strongly she felt. Smitten. They both loved chocolate pudding and macaroni and cheese from the box above all other foods. They could not take enough baths. Caitlin was bossy, but that suited Marie fine. Marie often felt herself in need of a leader.

Marie was pleasantly drunk the night Ellen and her French husband came home from the theater and found Marie passed out in the bathtub. She had put Caitlin to sleep and was watching bad television, a movie about a sexy teenaged babysitter. First the babysitter drugged the mother, then she seduced the father, and at the moment when Caitlin started to scream, she was chasing the daughter through the house, wielding a kitchen knife.

"Marie. Marie, Marie, Marie!"

Marie ran as fast as she could to Caitlin's room, crashing into an end table on the way, breaking a ceramic vase, afraid of everything: an intruder with a gun, a poisonous spider beneath the sheets, a monster in the closet. A raging fever. Knife-wielding babysitters.

But nothing was wrong.

Caitlin wanted to take a bath.

"You aren't sick?" Marie said, out of breath, trembling.

"You forgot my bath." Caitlin was standing up in her crib, holding on to the bars as if she were ready to revolt. "I feel sticky. I want my bath."

Caitlin was red from screaming. Marie was shaking with anger. Relief. She lifted Caitlin from the crib and discovered that the little girl was, in fact, sticky. Not only sticky, but visibly dirty. Her face was smeared with chocolate ice cream; they had eaten soft serve earlier that day. Marie put her finger on Caitlin's round, hot cheek.

"We forgot your bath?"

Though Marie was paid to take care of Caitlin, she often felt that Caitlin was looking after her. Marie always felt guilty for the things she did wrong. Every day there was some small new mistake to make, but so far, there had been no consequences. Marie smiled, feeling Caitlin's sturdy legs lock around her.

"I'm sorry, Caty Cat. You need a bath."

"I want a bath," Caitlin said.

"Good," Marie said. "So do I."

Marie carried Caitlin to the bathroom, passing through the living room to reclaim her drink, momentarily glancing at the TV set. The teenage babysitter, still wielding her knife, promised not to kill the girl if she came out of the closet. Marie continued walking; it was bath time, better than TV. Caitlin made happy gurgling sounds, pounding Marie's back like it was a drum.

Marie ran the water, Caitlin at her side, watching the water fill the tub.

"Bubbles," Caitlin said.

"Yes. Bubbles."

Marie generously poured Ellen's French lavender bubble bath beneath the running faucet. This was a secret between Marie and Caitlin; Ellen thought bubbles were bad for Caitlin's skin. When the tub was almost full, she took off Caitlin's damp white nightgown. Marie took a sip of what still remained of her drink, raised naked Caitlin high into the air from her armpits, and then dipped the bottom of Caitlin's feet into the water.

"Too hot," Caitlin said.

Marie nodded. This was part of their routine. Marie turned off the hot faucet, ran in only cold water, and then she lowered Caitlin back down.

"Better?" Marie said.

"Yes."

Caitlin grinned. Caitlin was happy when she got her way. She seemed to get her way most of the time. She would probably grow up into a disaster of a person: confident, arrogant, entitled—just like Ellen. Maybe, Marie thought, that was not entirely a bad thing.

"Let's try again, Kit Kat."

Marie lowered Caitlin back down into the tub. This time all the way in. Soon she would run more hot water. Marie was able to trick Caitlin this way every time. Caitlin reached for a yellow rubber duck and promptly smashed it over the head of another rubber duck. The tub was filled with bath toys.

"So violent," Marie observed.

Marie took off her clothes and got in, lying back against the opposite end. She reached for her drink. She took a deep sip of whiskey. She closed her eyes.

"Quack," she heard Caitlin say. "Quack quack quack."

It occurred to Marie that she was, at that particular

moment in time, happy. Happy. There weren't many times when Marie could remember feeling this way. Swimming in the ocean during those short, wonderful months in Mexico with Juan José. Making love. Taking walks under the stars. Planning their future, together. The babies they wanted to have. Marie had felt her life was exactly what it was supposed to be.

Marie was happy. It wasn't complicated. All it took was a bath. Caty Bean.

She opened her eyes, looked at naked Caitlin.

"Hi Caitlin," she said.

"This duck is so bad, Marie," Caitlin said.

"Get the duck," Marie said. She felt the lids of her eyes slide back shut.

"Bad duck," Caitlin said.

"Bad," Marie said. "Very bad."

Marie must have fallen asleep in the bath. She had not heard them come in, Ellen and her French husband, but somehow they were standing in the bathroom, fully dressed, staring. Ellen's mouth was open wide. She had those perfect teeth, the result of years of expensive orthodontics.

They were a stylish couple. Benoît Doniel was wearing a dark striped suit. His blue tie matched the color of Ellen's shimmery dress. Benoît Doniel was looking at Marie, looking at her naked. Benoît Doniel. Marie loved to say his name in her head. Benoît Doniel. Benoît Doniel. Benoît Doniel. It tasted good in her mouth, like chocolate. Like chocolate dipped in whiskey.

Since she had begun babysitting, Marie had managed to avoid contact with her employer's husband. Three weeks and not a single straight-on gaze. Benoît Doniel was not strikingly attractive. But he was sweet and sexy in a funny, self-deprecating kind of way. He wasn't tall; quite possibly he was short. Marie seemed to tower above him. His sandy brown hair fell into his eyes. He had also written Marie's absolute favorite novel in the world, *Virginie at Sea*, about a suicidal teenage girl who falls in love with a sick sea lion at the zoo.

Marie had kept her ardent love of Benoît's out-of-print book a secret. She had discovered a translated edition of the novel in the prison library. She'd read it again and again. Sometimes she would force herself to wait a day, sometimes two, and then Marie would start all over.

This was the real reason she was there. Why she had come to New York, arrived on Ellen's doorstep, asking for a job, though she had no idea at the time who Ellen had married. It was why she was naked in the bathtub, her body on display for Benoît Doniel's gaze. Marie's happiness wasn't about Caitlin, but the close proximity to Benoît Doniel, French novelist.

Now, at last, craning her neck out of the water, Marie allowed herself to look at him. Really look. She looked and looked. Benoît Doniel had a small mole on his cheek. His bottom teeth were crooked. His eyes were brown. She couldn't have known this, not from the black-and-white author photo. He was also grinning, grinning at Marie, unmistakably amused with the situation. He could not take his eyes off her. Marie held his gaze. Somehow, Ellen had married this amazing man, and now he was staring at Marie. Life had finally presented her with a gift.

"Hello there, Marie," Benoît Doniel said.

"Benoît." Marie rubbed her eyes. It was the first time she had spoken his name out loud. "Hello."

"Mommy and Daddy are home," Caitlin cried.

Caitlin kicked her legs, splashing water out of the tub. Ellen still had not spoken, but Caitlin's flailing seemed to stun her back into motion. She scooped her naked daughter from the tub and hugged her to her chest, soaking her blue dress.

"Jesus Christ, Marie," she said. "I pay you to babysit, not to take baths with my daughter, and certainly not to fall asleep in the tub. My God. I can't believe this."

Only then did Ellen notice the glass of whiskey balanced on the soap dish. The situation, at least, was interesting. Marie had no idea what Ellen would do. Ellen believed herself to be in control of her life.

Marie spread her legs open, not a lot, just enough.

"You're drinking? You're drunk? You were asleep in the fucking bathtub. You could have drowned my daughter. Did you lose all of your brain cells when you were in jail?"

"Down," Caitlin said. "Put me down."

Marie had locked eyes with Benoît Doniel.

There was no doubt at this point that he was staring at her. He pushed the hair out of his eyes to get a better look. Marie couldn't fathom how he had ended up with Ellen Kendall. She couldn't believe he was the same man who had written *Virginie at Sea*. He could have been writing about her, Marie, at sixteen. He had stolen her innermost thoughts, transcribed them word for word onto the page.

"Get out of the bathtub, Marie."

Marie was surprised to realize that Ellen was still in the bathroom. Marie couldn't be certain, but it seemed as if Ellen was screaming. It seemed as if her voice was much louder than it needed to be.

"Get out of the fucking bathtub. Get out. Get out."

"Mommy said 'fuck,' " Caitlin said.

Marie knew that she should get out of the tub. She understood that Ellen was at the point of explosion. But Marie was too invested in imagining the picture she made at that very moment. As if through Benoît Doniel's eyes. As if it were a scene in a movie. Marie was tall. She was thin. She had long, dark hair and surprisingly large breasts, which had always seemed out of proportion to the rest of her thin frame. Marie decided she would not move, not just yet. She would extend the moment as far as she could take it.

The next night, when she came home from the office, Ellen took Marie out to dinner.

Marie felt almost giddy with relief.

If Ellen was prepared to talk, if she was prepared to eat a meal with her, drink a drink, they could fix the situation. Pretend to forget what had happened the night before. Because when she thought about it, Marie knew she wasn't ready. She did not want to be in charge of her own life. She could wait for Benoît Doniel. She had seen how he looked at her. He would wait. He would flirt. They could take their time. Ellen had the capacity, not to forgive, but to forget.

When Marie had shown up at her doorstep three weeks ago, Ellen had greeted Marie as if nothing had happened. As if Marie hadn't spent the last six years in a medium-security prison for being an accessory to murder and bank robbery, six years in which Ellen had not once visited or written a letter. As if they hadn't had a colossal fight years before that, back in high school, after Marie had made the mistake of having sex with Ellen's boyfriend at the time, Harry Alford.

Marie loved Vietnamese food. She held open the door to the restaurant, pretending that there was nothing strange about the two of them, friends—old friends—going out for a meal. They had grown up next door to each other; Marie's mother had been the Kendalls' part-time housekeeper.

"I love this place," Marie said to Ellen.

Ellen grimaced.

Marie recognized this grimace, and suddenly she understood. The friendly invitation was a trap. A lie.

Ellen waited until after they ordered. Until after the waiter had brought their drinks, placed the delicious shrimp and vermicelli rolls in front of Marie. There had never been anything so good to eat in prison. On Chinese food night, they were served soggy egg rolls still dripping in oil.

"How was your day?" Elbows on the table, Ellen rested her chin on her folded hands. "Did you and Caitlin go to the park?"

Marie shook her head. "You know we went to the park. Just say it. Say whatever it is you are going to say to me."

"Okay." Ellen took a deep breath. "I made a mistake. You haven't changed. If anything, you've gotten worse. I don't know what I was thinking. To bring you into my home. To consider trusting you again. To entrust you with my child. I don't blame you, Marie. It's my fault. I blame myself. That I let this happen. Even when we were small, I knew something was wrong. I tried to convince myself that we were having fun, playing, but you were always waiting for snack time. You'd eat everything and ask for more."

"Your mother served good snacks," Marie said.

"Exactly," Ellen said. "You came for the snacks. My

mother told me to be generous. She said your father was dead, that your mother cleaned houses, that you had it hard."

Marie cupped her hand around her beer. Marie had had no idea. "She told you that?"

Marie had mistaken all the attention for kindness. They had pitied her. She used to sleep over on weekends, and Ellen's mother would tuck Marie in, kiss her on her forehead, pull the covers up to her chin.

"My house was nicer. You learned how to swim in our swimming pool. My mother would buy you books for Christmas. We fed you your first artichoke."

"And Brie," Marie said. "Don't forget. And lobster."

Marie had always wanted to be a Kendall, but when it came down to it, they had never wanted her. Not really. It had been a sadistic form of teasing, to let her into their home, to act as if she were part of the family, when she always received inferior birthday presents and was left behind when Ellen went away to summer camp.

Marie's mother had a PhD in Italian Renaissance Literature, but no practical job experience. Marie's father had died in a sailing accident when she was still a baby. What kind of piece of shit would do that, would get himself killed? That's what Marie's mother would say. Marie's mother rarely had anything nice to say.

Marie picked up a shrimp roll and put it back down.

"You never liked me," Ellen said. "You liked my house."

Marie hated being confronted with her childhood. This was the most direct Ellen had ever been with her and Marie did not like it. It was one thing for Marie to recognize her own disdain for Ellen; it was another thing to hear that it had always been mutual. Marie rolled her chopsticks back and forth between her hands, as if she could generate heat with the friction. She wanted Ellen to be afraid—to consider the possibility that Marie could stick one of these splintered wooden chopsticks right up into the meat of Ellen's eyeball.

"We were friends," Marie said.

Now, on the verge of being fired, Marie wanted to believe this. There was no reason that Ellen should have mistrusted Marie when they were little. Marie had been a perfectly unthreatening child. Ridiculously eager to please. She had also stolen Ellen's clothes, the occasional stuffed animal. Maybe Ellen had always known that. She had never let on.

"Come on, Marie. It was always obvious we were forced together. I know this sounds awful, but I'm not saying anything you don't already know. I've always had more advantages. And I was happy to share with you. I was. But you always had to take advantage of me. And then in high school, you slept with Harry. My boyfriend. There wasn't anything meaner you could have possibly done to me."

"He slept with me, too," Marie said.

The distinction seemed important. Harry Alford had taken Marie's hand, led her upstairs, and fucked Marie on the floor of a walk-in closet of the master bedroom at their high school graduation party. He didn't love her, of course. He loved Ellen. It was a little like Ellen's mother, all over again. Marie had large breasts, even then.

"I don't even know what I am doing sitting in a restaurant with you," Ellen said. "Let alone inviting you into my home. I must have been out of my mind."

"He was a creep, you know that," Marie said, surprised that she was defending herself. She never had before. It had always been understood, before, that Marie had done a bad

thing. Because she was Marie. Jealous and needy. The girl
next door. Because she could not help herself. "I was drunk.
He didn't talk to me the next day. He acted as if nothing had
ever happened. Do you know how that made me feel?"

"I can't believe that I forgave you," Ellen said.

"You never forgave me," Marie said.

Ellen shook her head.

"We are sitting here right now," Ellen said. "I am paying
for your dinner. I forgave you. Don't contradict me. I know
what forgiveness is. You went to jail, Marie, and when you got
out, I gave you a job. I gave you a job. Watching my daughter.
My daughter. Do you understand what a big deal that was for
me? How precious Caitlin is to me? I trusted you."

"Pfff," Marie said, for lack of a better word.

It had been a surprise to Marie, too. She had no babysitting
experience. They had all that history. Clearly Ellen was trying
to prove something, if not to Marie, then to herself. Marie,
however, did not care what Ellen's motivations had been.

Ellen had also wanted Marie to clean, to dust and do
laundry, make beds, but Marie had refused. "I am not my
mother. I won't be your maid," she had said.

It turned out that Marie had no ambition, but she did have
pride. Ellen backed down. Ellen had never trusted Marie; she
needed a servant.

As far as Marie was concerned, the conversation was over.
She did not need to hear what Ellen had to say next. Best of
luck. Let's stay in touch. Marie lay her chopsticks down at the
table. There were those uneaten shrimp rolls staring at her.
Could she get them to go? Ellen's contempt for Marie was
clear. She did not trust Marie with her daughter. There was
nothing left to talk about.

It was time for Marie to get up, leave the table, leave before the rest of the food came, even though she had ordered all of her favorite dishes. Her nice and easy days with Caitlin—taking baths, taking naps, walks in the park—that was over. Done. Marie knew that later, when she was alone, she would start to feel it. No more Caitlin. Marie could not imagine. She woke up in her basement room each day, eager to get upstairs, share Caitlin's organic Cheerios.

Leave, she told herself.

But Marie did not get up. She wasn't ready to admit defeat. She still wanted Caitlin. She still wanted that refrigerator full of food. And she wanted Benoît Doniel. Fate had delivered him to Marie.

"Do you have anything to say for yourself?" Ellen said. "Can you explain what I walked in on last night?"

Ellen stared at her, across the table, waiting. A response seemed to be required. Marie yawned. She stabbed a spring roll with her chopstick, digging a hole in its perfect center.

"Am I boring you?" Ellen said.

"I'm bored out of my fucking mind."

"How do you expect me to act?" Ellen grabbed the chopstick from Marie's hand. "You think I should be nice? I trusted you. I trusted you, and you fucked me over. You can't handle a job meant for a teenager. My mother always thought so much of you. She thought we let you down. When you ended up in jail, she felt responsible."

This was news to Marie. Ellen's parents had retired, moved to Arizona, and they had not kept in touch. Like Ellen, her mother had not written to Marie all that time she spent in prison. Six years. She could have sent something. A book to read. A tin of brownies. A letter would have been enough, a show of support. A small kindness. Marie had never committed a crime. She had fallen in love with a bank robber.

"I gave you this job against my better judgment. I'm really busy at work, Marie. I have an important job. I have a career, Marie. I swear to God, I don't have time to look for a new nanny right now."

"I've inconvenienced you," Marie said, wondering what the fuck Ellen was talking about. Ellen was worried about her job. Marie was going to wreck her marriage. Marie might have held off, had she been allowed to keep her job. She would have put off the inevitable. "I apologize. It must be hard to find good help."

"We can be adult about this," Ellen said. "Caitlin is fine. I know that. She seems to like you."

"She seems to."

"You don't have to leave right away. We can be professional about this. I am probably going to need at least a week to find someone else. I've contacted an agency, but it takes a little while. That should give you some time to figure out your next step."

Ellen hailed a waiter and asked for a new set of chopsticks. It was typical for Ellen to act decisively, without mercy, and then expect something in return. But Marie would *work* for another week. It would be enough time.

"Look, Marie, I'll lend you money if you need it," Ellen said. "It's not like I want you out on the street. I'm sure your mother would let you move home."

Marie shook her head, speechless.

Go home to her mother.

She hadn't spoken to her mother in the six years she had been in prison. She had no plans to do so now.

"I have to feel safe," Ellen continued. "I can't concentrate at work if I'm convinced that you might kill my little girl."

Marie started to laugh.

"Jesus, Ellen, you can't feel safe," she said. "Not ever. Not for a second. You can die crossing the street. You should be afraid of terrorists. Pedophiles in the park. Natural disasters, you should be fucking scared of that."

"She could have drowned," Ellen said.

"She didn't drown."

"She could have drowned."

"She didn't drown."

"My husband is not interested in you."

"Your husband." There it was. At last. "Benoît Doniel."

Marie could feel herself blush, the heat spreading across her cheeks, just from saying his name. She had had a dream about him that afternoon, napping during Caitlin's nap time. Marie could remember specific, erotic details.

"I'll say it again," Ellen said. "In case you are thinking about trying a second Harry. My husband is not interested in you."

"No, of course he isn't."

"Benoît thinks that you are immature."

This interested Marie. Why immature? Was that all that he had said? What hadn't he said? They had talked about her. Was Ellen testing her husband with Marie? She was out of her mind, taking a risk like that.

"Of course I am immature. Look at my sneakers."

Marie raised her leg onto the table, displaying her purple canvas high-tops. She had missed her sneakers when she was in prison. Ellen frowned. A waiter appeared at the table, hovering with a tray of food. He also frowned at Marie, her purple

Converse All Stars on the table. Marie could smell the crispy squid. Marie loved crispy squid.

Marie put her foot down so that the waiter would serve the food. They still hadn't touched their shrimp rolls. She stared at the fresh plates of steaming hot food, almost helpless before it. She would be unable to make a heroic gesture. She would have to eat everything, drink her beer, order another. She would let Ellen pay for her meal.

She would not regret it.

That was how Marie wanted to live her life. Without regret.

"My husband thinks you are immature," Ellen repeated. "And without soul. Those are his words."

Marie wondered what she was supposed to say. It occurred to her that perhaps Benoît Doniel was telling Ellen exactly what she wanted to hear. Or maybe it was true. It was possible that Marie did not have a soul. She had had this same thought on her own. Benoît Doniel was a gifted novelist and perhaps an excellent judge of character. But that could not begin to explain his marriage to Ellen, such a hard and inflexible woman. She was all wrong for him. She was certainly no Virginie; she had been a picture-perfect, well-adjusted teenage girl.

"I don't care what your husband thinks about me," Marie said.

"That's good to know," Ellen said. "Not that it matters what you think. Let's get this straight. For this upcoming week, you can't drink in my home. You can't bathe with Caitlin. You do not talk to my husband. I'm going to repeat the last one. You do not talk to my husband. These are my rules. These rules are, I believe, more than fair."

And then, as if something amicable had actually been settled between them, Ellen began to eat.

Marie watched Ellen bite into her shrimp roll, angry that Ellen had gotten to taste the food first. "Understood. No drinking. No bathing. No looking at your spouse."

Marie was perfectly at ease lying to Ellen's face. Of course, she would continue to drink in Ellen's apartment. She would continue to take baths with Caitlin, and she would also look at Benoît Doniel and talk to Benoît Doniel as much as she possibly could. She would do more, much more than talk. Marie could feel her confidence returning.

"Marie, you probably won't believe me," Ellen said. "But I still care about you. In our twisted way, I think we are friends. Maybe we can learn from this experience. I don't think it was ever comfortable for either of us, this situation, your living in my home. My giving you orders. You are not good at following orders."

Marie saluted.

Ellen ignored her.

"I want you to know that you can still see Caitlin. If you decide to stay in New York. If you can afford to stay. If you get another job in the city. I guess it might be difficult with your police record."

"With my police record," Marie said, grinning.

Ellen, of course, couldn't help herself; she had to bring up Marie's police record. It was her last and best weapon. It trumped all other episodes from Marie's past. Ellen didn't understand Marie in the slightest. She assumed that they viewed life the same way because they came from the same town and had gone to a Bruce Springsteen concert together when they were thirteen. She didn't understand that taunting Marie about prison was useless, because Marie was not embarrassed. Or ashamed. Marie had never felt any regret.

She had been in love. Wildly, madly, thoughtlessly, heedlessly in love. When Juan José had shown up at her door, desperate, covered in blood, when he had told her that he had made it out of the bank, but his partner hadn't been so lucky, that the police were searching for him, she'd run off without a moment's hesitation and she had never looked back.

Later, once they were on the road, Marie had learned that Juan José's partner had killed one of the security guards. But still, Marie hadn't allowed herself any doubts. Juan José had not killed anyone and Marie wanted to be wherever Juan José was. In his bed. In his house, with his mother and sisters and squawking chickens underfoot. Juan José used to recite poetry to Marie in Spanish. He had taken her dancing. They would have sex before they went dancing. They had had sex after they went dancing. Marie had felt alive in a way she had never felt before.

That had been worth going to jail for.

Marie helped herself to the crispy squid. To jasmine rice and the sautéed greens. A delicious shrimp roll. She started to eat. The squid was still hot. She had a week. An entire week.

"I can front you five hundred dollars," Ellen said. "Consider it severance pay."

"That would be great," Marie said.

Marie would take the money. She would take a whole lot more than that.

Marie had spent only six of her thirty years in prison,
but often she found herself overwhelmed by her newly re-
gained freedom. Marie had not yet gotten used to the swing
of life. She hadn't, in fact, minded jail nearly as much as she'd
thought she would.

Her days in prison were ridiculously clear. She ate three
meals a day, always at the same appointed time, in the same
airless cafeteria, seated in the same place at the end of a long
table. She had a job in the prison laundry. The work was surprisingly difficult, more physically challenging than anything
she had ever done before. Marie learned how to operate indus-
trial machinery that sent enormous quantities of prison sheets
and blankets and towels and uniforms through a long, danger-
ously hot iron.

Marie had even made friends with another woman who
worked in the laundry. Ruby Hart was in for twenty-two
years; she had killed her husband, hitting him strategically in

the head with a hot iron. She did not regret killing Hector. "Otherwise," she had said, matter-of-factly, "I would be dead." And she added, "It felt good. Hitting it to that mother-fucker where it hurt."

Ruby Hart appreciated the irony of her work assignment. She had not meant to kill him.

All of the killers Marie met in prison had killed for a good reason. Marie, of course, had not killed anyone, but the other prisoners had not held this against Marie. It was nothing like jail on television.

Ruby taught Marie how to fold T-shirts with a technique she had once learned working at the Gap, the job she had had before she had been incarcerated for murder. They worked well together, loading and unloading innumerable washers and dryers, running hot irons. Ruby seemed to believe in life after prison. She studied law while Marie reread *Virginie at Sea*.

"Prepare for your future," Ruby used to tell her.

The truth was, nothing bad ever happened to Marie in prison. She had never been attacked. She had never felt herself to be in any physical danger. She felt competent and strong. She gained muscle from working in the laundry; she also lost the weight she'd put on in college. Even with the hours she put in at the laundry, Marie still had time on weekends to walk the prison grounds, to read in her cell. For the first time in her life, free from the need to make any sort of decision, Marie felt herself relax.

Jail had been a better, more instructive time in her life than both college and high school. Sometimes, staring into Ellen's refrigerator, the drawers and closets full of clothes, jewelry, confronted with so many choices, Marie missed it.

Even though he did not have a job, Benoît Doniel left every
morning for work. He had an office, a small cubicle, somewhere downtown in some communal writers' space. He was
hard at work on his second novel. Marie knew these things.
She had heard him talk to Ellen about good writing days,
bad ones. He would get angry when Ellen pressured him
with questions about his work.

For as long as she had been Caitlin's nanny, he was gone
six hours a day, every day, but Marie wasn't surprised when
he came home early the day after Marie had been fired, back
in time for Caitlin's lunch.

Benoît drank the coffee Marie offered him out of a blue
bowl. He happily accepted a second blue bowl full of macaroni
and cheese. He ate with delight, spooning in extra butter. He
was ridiculously French. The extra butter, the coffee in a bowl,
his accent. To further prove his Frenchness, Benoît smoked
while he ate. Caitlin imitated her father, taking drags from a

baby carrot. Marie leaned back in her chair, watching them both.

Lunch. A threesome. A family. Benoît smoked. He sipped his coffee. He knew how to linger over a meal. At one point, he leaned over across the table to touch Caitlin's cheek. This pleased Marie.

Nothing had happened, but it would. Soon. Marie knew this. She was provocatively dressed: a short red cotton skirt, a white tank top with lace at the top, cleavage exposed. Because she had known he would come. She had expected him and she wanted her flesh in abundant display. The macaroni and cheese was warm and creamy in her mouth. She looked at Benoît and made no effort to mask her desire. All that time, three long weeks, Marie had been careful not to attract Benoît's attention. Her behavior had bordered on rude. She had made a heroic effort.

"Look at how comfortable we are," Marie said.

She waved her arms, embracing the room—the sunlight streaming in through the window, Caitlin with her baby carrots.

"The three of us."

"We've never talked before," Benoît said. "Not all this time, when you live in my home, take care of my daughter. I see you talking with Caitlin constantly, nonstop talk, jabber jabber jabber, but never with me. We don't talk. I look at you and you look away. I wonder, why? Why don't you talk to me?"

Marie put both hands around her mug of coffee.

"I wonder."

It dawned on her that Benoît had been avoiding her for the very same reason she had avoided him. She had not been invisible. They had *known* not to talk each other. They were good people who both suffered from lapses in acceptable behavior.

"I cannot remember," Benoît said. "Why did you not come to our wedding? You're Ellen's oldest friend. Why didn't I meet you until now?"

Marie shook her head. "She didn't tell you?" Marie was not surprised. Of course Ellen would not want to talk about her. "I was in jail when you got married."

Benoît put out his cigarette and immediately lit another. Caitlin pounded her fist against her high table.

"Me," Caitlin cried. "Feed me."

"Yes, of course." Benoît absently stuck a spoon of macaroni and cheese into Caitlin's chin.

"No," she said. "My mouth. My mouth. Silly Daddy."

Caitlin, of course, knew how to feed herself. She opened her mouth wide and Benoît tried again.

"You were in jail." Benoît took a puff of his cigarette, a sip of his coffee, another bite of macaroni and cheese. "You went to jail? For robbing a bank? Ellen mentioned this, just last night. But I have trouble believing this story. It seems, I don't know, out of character?"

"Ellen never told you what happened to me?"

"Ellen said very little about you. Just one day, she fires Bertha, who she was perhaps a little unhappy with, and she gives you her job. But now, as I understand, you no longer work here, live here. The rules, I think, they change." Benoît shrugged. "I like my life. Here. This city. This room. My American wife. This little girl." He waved, just like Marie, to embrace the room, his daughter Caitlin, the blue bowl of coffee in front of him. "I really don't care to fight. Ellen, you know, is quick to fight. So I did not ask questions. But now, now I am curious. About you. Marie. I love that name. Marie."

"What do you want to know?" Marie asked him. She decided, then and there, she would tell Benoît everything. "I will tell you everything," she told him.

Marie sat on her hands, resisting the overwhelming urge to touch him. Not yet. Soon. But not yet.

And then, she touched him anyway. Stroked the top of the palm of his hand. Benoît shivered. Caitlin was smoking her carrot stick.

"Did you rob a bank?"

Marie shook her head. "My boyfriend robbed a bank. A small one. In the suburbs. Juan José. He was only twenty-two years old. He was this perfect boy. Like a painting. I wasn't much older, twenty-four. I didn't know he was going to rob a bank. I knew almost nothing about him, really. I had met him in a bar, the week before. He showed up in the middle of the night at my door. Scared. Bleeding. I didn't even think about it. He needed me. We went to Mexico. Later, after the police found us, I went to jail. I didn't regret it. I don't."

Benoît stared at Marie. He looked down at the hand that had touched him. He put down his cigarette to brush the hair from his eyes. "Where is he now?"

Marie looked away. She could not look at Benoît Doniel and answer this question. Marie wanted to tell Benoît everything, but she couldn't trust herself to say the answer out loud. She was, she supposed, an accumulation of the events of her life. She had no reason to lie, not to this particular man. It was real, what was happening between them in the kitchen, the bright afternoon sunlight streaming in from the kitchen window. Marie would tell Benoît the truth, give him a piece of her sorrow. She would offer her story as if it were a gift.

"He hanged himself," she said. "In prison."

"*Merde,*" Benoît said.

Sitting on the chair, Marie brought her knees up to her chest. She kissed her knee.

"I understand," he said. "About that kind of loss."

Marie allowed herself to look, again, at Benoît.

"My sister," Benoît said.

He lit a fresh cigarette. Marie waited. Caitlin stuck out her tongue.

"My little sister. My *petite sœur*. Nathalie. She killed herself."

They were no longer grinning, Marie and Benoît. The sky, as if in tacit cooperation with the change in mood, had turned gray. Marie had never found out what had driven Juan José to kill himself. She suspected that his actions had forever damaged her. Marie had promised to wait for him. She had been explicitly clear.

"She was a poet," Benoît said. "So sensitive."

"Me," Caitlin said. "Talk to me me me."

"You," Benoît said.

"Me," Caitlin said.

"You," Marie said.

Caitlin threw her empty bowl of macaroni on the floor. It bounced, but did not break.

"Now look, *ma petite*," Benoît said. "I can have lunch with you and I can also talk to Marie. We are having an interesting conversation. You smoke your carrot, drink your apple juice, and listen quietly. Like a good girl."

Benoît put Caitlin's red sippy cup into her hand.

"Me!"

Caitlin threw the red sippy cup on the floor.

"Me!"

Her small face turned red.

Marie was impressed with Caitlin's tantrum. There was no reason for her to behave. Benoît was invading her territory. Maybe Caitlin couldn't understand Marie's conversation with Benoît, but she was smart enough to be jealous.

Benoît Doniel was actively appraising Marie, registering the new information about her past, while taking in the present-day Marie, in her short red cotton skirt and equally revealing tank top, her abundant cleavage. Their attraction, clearly, was about more than shared grief.

"Me!" Caitlin screamed. "Me! Me!"

"Enough," Benoît Doniel said to his small daughter. "Enough of this me business." He shook his head. "You are hurting my ears. You are becoming irritating."

Caitlin wouldn't have it. It was her lunch, the lunch she had every day alone with Marie. Her Marie. Marie understood Caitlin's frustration. She was not surprised when Caitlin started to cry, though she also had never seen her behave like that before.

Benoît sighed. He got up from the table and picked her up, but Caitlin only began to wail louder, her arms and legs flailing. "No, no, no. Down. Caitlin down."

"Hey, hey," Benoît said. "What is this? No tantrums."

He looked at Marie, confused. "Does she need a nap? Do you think?"

Marie shook her head.

"No," Caitlin said. "No. No. No nap."

"What is it, Kit Kat?" Marie asked. "What do you need right now?"

"A bath," Caitlin said. "I want to take bath."

"You do?" Marie said. "A bath? Really?"

Caitlin had stopped struggling in Benoît's grasp. Marie held Benoît's gaze. His eyes were sparkling. Marie remembered the dream she'd had the day before. It had taken place in the bathtub. Marie was pleased by how easy they were all making it for her: Caitlin, Ellen, Benoît.

Marie slid her finger under the strap of her white tank top, pulled it down past her shoulder, holding Benoît's gaze.

"I want to take a bath!" Caitlin yelled.

"You know," Benoît said. "I am not against the idea. A bath might be rather pleasant."

"Bath," Caitlin said. "Yes, yes, yes, yes."

"Caitlin and I like to take baths together," Marie said.

"This I know," Benoît said. "I have a beautiful picture." He touched his forehead. "Inside my head."

"And that is why you are here now?" Marie said.

Marie was sure, but she wanted to be absolutely sure. Before she went into the bathroom and took off the little bit of clothing she was wearing. Three weeks of virtue. Over. It was an enormous relief. "Because of this beautiful picture in your head?"

"Isn't that ridiculously obvious?" Benoît said.

Marie reached out her hand, and Benoît pulled her from her chair.

"Stop talking," Caitlin said.

Marie leaned over, scooped Caitlin from Benoît and took her into her arms. A week from now, this smart, funny, obnoxious, beautiful, wonderful little girl would be leading a life separate from Marie. Caitlin had not been informed of her mother's imperial decree. She had no idea what was happening to her; she had no say about her own fate.

Marie didn't want to think about leaving Caitlin.

She wanted Benoît.

She wanted him naked and soapy, tangled and wet in her arms. She wanted him to read to her. To read *Virginie at Sea*.

"A bath," Marie said.

Marie carried Caitlin to the bathroom as if nothing unusual was happening. Benoît followed directly behind, his hands gently cupping Marie's waist.

The bathtub was large and deep, but it seemed smaller with Benoît Doniel in it. The water came from a spout in the wall in the center of the tub. Marie and Benoît were both able to lie back on opposite ends, Marie's longer legs bent and then extended over Benoît's. They pushed Caitlin back and forth between them like a rubber ball.

Caitlin was delighted. She laughed and she laughed. When Marie had Caitlin on her side of the tub, she caressed Benoît Doniel's penis gently with her foot. Benoît rubbed the inside of Marie's thigh with his big toe.

"Again!" Caitlin screamed. "Again! Again!"

After the bath, Marie brought Caitlin into her room, and put her down for a nap.

"I am very, very tired," Caitlin said, her voice serious.

"You go to sleep," Marie said. "I'll be here when you wake up."

Marie kissed Caitlin on top of her damp head. This could

be her last moment with Caitlin. She had to keep that in mind.
If Ellen had a brain in her head, she would not last a full day
at her office. But Ellen would no sooner leave work early than
she would have cut class. Marie felt the temptation to find
her clothes, lace her sneakers, and leave, leave now, with the
author of *Virginie at Sea* waiting for her in the bedroom,
wanting her.

To get out before it started.

This was not the equivalent of a trip to Mexico.

It wasn't.

"Sleep," Marie repeated, and she was amazed, because
that was what Caitlin did.

Caitlin never fell asleep this easily. Marie watched her tiny
chest rise and fall, amazed not only by the way Caitlin was co-
operating, but how the child had practically orchestrated the
afternoon to suit Marie's purposes. Marie opened the sash of
Ellen's robe, a gorgeous red silk kimono she had been eyeing
for several weeks. This was a fine time for it. She looked down
at Caitlin, for another second longer, wondering why she was
waiting, when she knew exactly what she wanted.

Marie walked purposefully to the master bedroom. Benoît
Doniel lay naked on the bed. His bed. Ellen's bed. He saw
Marie and smiled. In that brief moment, while Benoît waited
for Marie to lie down next to him, Marie thought of many
different things she could say. Her mind raced. In the end, she
didn't say a thing.

It was unfortunate that Benoît Doniel was married to
Ellen. Marie was certain that this was not the cause of her attraction. This was not high school; he was no Harry Alford.
Benoît Doniel had written Marie's favorite book in the entire
world, the book that had seen her through six years in jail, had

become a secret source of solace. Of pleasure. He was a rock star. Her soul mate.

"The babysitter," Benoît said.

"The husband."

They understood each other, the situation. Marie let Ellen's kimono drop to the floor.

The next afternoon, it happened again.

And the day after that.

And the day after that.

And the day after that.

Benoît Doniel left the apartment in the morning, same as always, but returned not long after Ellen went to work. He joined Marie and Caitlin on their morning walks. They came back, lounged on the living-room floor, watched *Sesame Street*, played with Caitlin's toys. Benoît even helped Marie with her work, making them lunch. He made ham and egg sandwiches on baguettes. Because he was French. The sandwiches pleased Marie enormously; they were so good that Marie found herself wanting Benoît even more.

After lunch, the three of them went to the neighborhood playground together. Benoît spoke French to the nannies from Haiti. He pushed Caitlin on the swings. "This is a nice life," he said. "I wonder why I'm not her nanny."

"Aren't you writing a book?" Marie said. "How is that going?"

Benoît did not answer this. Instead, he shrugged his shoulders. Marie understood how he might be having a hard time; how could he hope to write something as good as *Virginie at Sea* ever again? Why should he be required to? Why was success required of a person? And once you were successful, life required you to do it again and again.

I love your book, Marie thought, but did not say.

Benoît was having an affair. Marie was not sure what she was having.

After the playground, they went back to the brownstone and took their baths. Caitlin was a clean and happy child.

On their fifth day, Marie surprised herself by crying when they made love. Every moment, in bed, at the park, in the bathtub, was tinged with nostalgia. Benoît did not ask Marie for an explanation; she opened her eyes as Benoît Doniel licked her tears away to see that Benoît was also crying.

"This is happening to you, too, isn't it?" Marie said.

Marie had not told Benoît about *Virginie at Sea*. Therefore, he had had no idea what he meant to her. But maybe, already, it was about more than sex. Maybe he might love Marie, too. That was what she wanted. Benoît went back down beneath the covers. He started at Marie's calves, kissing and gently biting, and then worked his way up. She felt herself falling hopelessly in love.

Again.

"*Je t'aime,*" Benoît said.

Marie was certain that was what she heard, though the words were muffled. *Je t'aime.* He couldn't have said that. She would leave, and his life would not be what it was before. He would continue to sleep with Ellen in this bed, but he would remember what it was like with Marie. Marie had exposed a gaping hole in his life. He would miss her.

Benoît bit into her thigh. Hard. Marie slapped the back of his head.

"Asshole," she said.

Ellen pulled the plug two days early.

She approached Marie in the kitchen. Marie was giving Caitlin her breakfast, organic Cheerios and apple juice. She hadn't yet seen Benoît Doniel, but had heard his footsteps in the hall. Marie knew that he was in the shower. She always knew where he was.

Ellen placed five crisp one-hundred-dollar bills onto the kitchen table.

"The service found another sitter to start on Monday," Ellen said.

"Oh," Marie said, focusing her gaze on the money. "Do you need me this weekend?"

"We can take it from here. Thanks for giving me this time. But I'd like for you to leave this weekend. I'm sorry that it had to end this way," Ellen said. Her voice was not sorry at all.

Caitlin swallowed a spoonful of cereal. She smiled at Marie.

"Hi Marie," Caitlin said.

"Hi Caty Bean," Marie said.

It often unnerved Marie how happy Caitlin appeared to be. She was too young to know about imminent doom.

"Hi Marie," Caitlin said, waving her spoon.

"Hi Caty Bean," Marie said.

Ellen had her hands on her hips.

"Anyway, like I said, the new nanny starts next week. I hope you've made other arrangements. You could go home. To your mother."

Marie said nothing. She could not go home. To her mother. Her mother, who had expected Marie to pay rent to sleep in her own bedroom when she returned after graduating from college. Who had refused to pay for a real lawyer after she was arrested. Who had failed to pick her up at the prison gates on the day of her release. It had stunned Marie, her mother's lack of compassion. Marie looked at Caitlin, eating her Cheerios with her fingers. She wondered what she would not forgive this little girl.

"I have to get to work," Ellen said. "Benoît promised to come home early, so you can start packing."

"Hi Marie," Caitlin said.

Marie smiled at Caitlin. She smoothed the money in the palm of her hand. Crisp new bills. Marie folded the money, put it in the back pocket of her jeans. It was an insult, to think that going back home to her mother was Marie's only option. She was much more capable than that. Ellen always underestimated Marie.

"Hi Caitlin," she said, this time an afterthought.

"Hi."

"Don't think I don't know how you operate," Ellen said.

"You do? Know how I operate? Do you?"

Marie had begun to doubt Ellen's intelligence. Ellen was smart in specific, measurable, obvious ways; she had gotten good grades at well-established institutions of learning, she was able to get a so-called good job and to keep this job, to earn enormous sums of money. Maybe these were admirable qualities. But Ellen had no insight into people. She had had the amazing fortune of marrying Benoît Doniel, the world's most attractive, underappreciated living French author. But was she grateful? Was she appreciative? Did she try each and every day to deserve him? No. Ellen was standing there, in her own light-filled, beautiful kitchen, giving money to the woman who was fucking her husband. She had no idea. She never did.

It almost made Marie feel sorry for her.

"Don't think about stealing my clothes," Ellen said. "And don't take any of my jewelry. Not even a book. I'm serious. I want to find every object in place after you're gone. I know where every single thing is."

Marie grinned.

"I hate that," Ellen said. "You're mocking me with that smile."

But Marie couldn't stop. The grin was involuntary. It turned into a nervous laugh, loud, almost hysterical. Nothing was funny. Caitlin started laughing, too.

Ellen bit her lip.

"I want to slap you," she said.

"So slap me," Marie said, covering her mouth. She had gotten the hiccups. She hiccupped.

"I want to," Ellen said.

"Then slap me. You have plenty of reasons."

Ellen looked confused.

Marie hiccupped again.

"I almost drowned your child, right? I slept with Harry Alford. There's always that. It was more than ten years ago and he got me drunk. But still. You should probably hit me for that. Oh, what else? I wear your kimono. The red silk one."

Marie stopped there. She did not want to go too far.

Ellen started to shake. Her entire body was shaking.

"You're right. We haven't been friends for a long time," Marie said. "You never liked me. I was your mother's charity case. She always compared us and you came out ahead. I never had a chance. You could be grateful for that alone. Anyway, you better hit me. This is your big chance. Tomorrow, I'll be gone."

Ellen slapped Marie. Hard. Marie felt a slow burn spread across her face. She had no idea what would happen next, but she felt exultant. Ellen really thought she had it all: happiness, a family, security. She thought she was *entitled*. Marie put her hand to her burning cheek, and she watched, silent, as Ellen picked up her purse, reached for her keys, and headed for the door. The idiot did not even give Caitlin a thoughtless peck on the head; she didn't even pause at the door to look back, say good-bye.

Marie watched Ellen go, impatient.

Only then could she figure out what was hers to take.

"I love my wife," Benoît Doniel told her.

"Sure you do," Marie said. "It's obvious."

She tucked a lock of Caitlin's wispy white-blond hair behind her ear. They had taken Caitlin to the Central Park Zoo. Benoît had made his trademark French baguette sandwiches and wrapped them in tin foil. They had bars of milk chocolate. Miniature bottles of Orangina. It was their last day. Their first and last real outing. Benoît had proposed something special to see her off.

Marie was furious. She would not be sent off. Not by him, too. There they were, standing in front of the sea lion tank, watching the sea lions go round and round. The day itself was grim, a steady drizzle coming from the sky, dark clouds overhead.

"I did not marry her for the money, if that's what you think," Benoît said.

"I didn't say a thing."

"Actually, I might have. A little bit. I saw her in Paris for the first time, drinking a Diet Coke and looking out onto the Seine, and I thought, this woman, she can save me. She was staying at an expensive hotel. In St. Michel."

"But you love her," Marie said. "That's what you feel the need to tell me. Right now. That you love your wife."

"I do."

Marie did not believe him. But even knowing that it was a lie, she would have preferred that Benoît had not divulged this bit of information. Ellen was going to win again; she always won, even though Marie wasn't in competition.

Marie always lost. Ellen went to graduate school. Marie went to a medium-security correctional center. Benoît Doniel, however, hadn't been a contest. Marie did not want Benoît because he belonged to Ellen. She wanted him because of the baguette sandwiches. She wanted him because of the sex in the afternoon. She wanted him because of *Virginie at Sea*. Because of *Virginie at Sea*, the book that had soothed her soul through six years of prison. It had been her favorite thing in the entire world. He had written that. Marie was awestruck with the idea that an actual person could do that. This was not about revenge. Marie needed Benoît Doniel. She loved him.

And he needed her. He loved her.

That's what Marie decided.

Someone had to make the decisions. In Marie's last relationship, Juan José had taken the initiative, robbing the bank, asking her to run away with him. Benoît seemed to require help.

"It's funny," Benoît said, staring straight ahead, breaking the long silence. "That you chose to come here today."

"Why?" Marie said, though she knew exactly what was funny. "Funny how?"

Two sea lions shot up from the water. Caitlin clapped her hands.

"Look, Marie, look!"

"Sea lions," Marie said.

Marie pressed her hands against the tank and Caitlin did the same thing.

"Sea lions," Caitlin said.

"Aren't they beautiful?"

"Yes," Caitlin said, and then she started to scream. "Yes! Yes! Yes!"

It was the one thing that Caitlin would do that Marie did not like. Scream. Marie shook her head.

"Quiet, Caty Bean."

The sea lions disappeared back underwater. Seconds later, they sprang up again. One sea lion landed on the large rock formation in the center of the pool. The sea lion arched its back, and then seemed to change its mind, slipping back into the water.

"Why is it funny?" Marie asked Benoît again, forcing him to talk to her. They had had only that one actual conversation, really, in the kitchen, when he told her about his dead sister. "Tell me. Why?"

Benoît Doniel pushed his swoopy hair out of his eyes.

Marie ran her fingertips over her earrings. They were small good hoops, Ellen's earrings. She had been robbing Ellen all along, every day, from the cheese and the whiskey to the kimono and the earrings. She had slipped more than one twenty-dollar bill from Ellen's wallet.

Still, Benoît did not answer the question.

Caitlin began to run around the circumference of the tank, chasing down the swimming sea lions.

"Maybe," Marie said, finally, speaking for him, because she couldn't wait anymore. Because they were running out of time. Today would be the day Ellen came home from work early. At some point it would actually dawn on her that Marie really was not to be trusted. Ellen had been right about that.

"Maybe," Marie said again, looking at Caitlin, who had stopped running and was pressing her hands against the glass tank. "Maybe you think it's funny we are here because you wrote a book called *Virginie at Sea*. A beautiful book about an angry girl in love with a sick sea lion. She visits the sea lion whenever anything goes wrong in her life. She visits the sea lion when anything good happens in her life. She loves the sea lion more than anyone or anything. And now, here we are, in the midst of a major crisis in your life, looking at sea lions."

Understanding began to dawn on Benoît's face. Marie had always liked this face, even before they had met, from the photo on the back cover of his book. The swoopy hair in the eyes. The mischievous expression. Marie opened her backpack and pulled out her weathered copy of *Virginie at Sea*, never returned to the prison library, the paperback cover laminated, the spine tagged with a yellow call number.

"Maybe you should sign this," she said. "Before I go."

Benoît took the book from Marie's hand.

"Look at this," he said. "*Mon Dieu*. You have this. I had no idea. You read this? You did? Thank you. I don't believe this. You always surprise me, Marie. Oh my God. Marie."

Marie loved the sound of Benoît Doniel saying her name. He had turned it into something special. Her name became something French.

"I love this book," Marie said. "This is my favorite book of all books. *Virginie at Sea*."

"It is?" Benoît said. "You love it? *Vraiment?* You do?"

"I do."

"I didn't know. I had no idea."

"I'm telling you now."

"This is crazy," Benoît said. "I love my wife."

"That's what you said."

"I do."

"You don't." Marie reached for Benoît's hands. "You are scared. You feel guilty. You feel affection for Ellen. Gratitude. I understand. You might have loved her, a long time ago. Not anymore. You love me."

"This is covered in plastic," Benoît said, removing his hands from Marie's, putting the book against Marie's cheek. "The book. Why?"

"I got it from the library. When I was in prison. They laminated the books to protect them."

"They have copies of *Virginie at Sea* in American jails?"

Marie had thought it was a miracle, too. To have found a book that made her so happy, night after night, in her prison cell. She could not explain, either, how life had led her straight to him, Benoît Doniel, the writer, the actual person, and also to Caitlin, wondrous Caitlin, who had resumed chasing the sea lions.

Marie took Benoît's hands again. This time he let her.

"I don't love my wife?" he said.

Benoît was waiting for Marie to answer. Instead, she kissed him. Hands in his hair, body pressed against him. In the zoo, in front of the sea lions. And Benoît Doniel, who might or might not love his wife, returned this kiss with equal force.

"Look!" Caitlin screamed.

They pulled away from each other. Benoît blinked. There was a sea lion in front of them, on top of the rock, arching its head up to the sun, which was coming out from behind the clouds.

"You remind me of my sister," Benoît said.

"Nathalie?"

"Yes."

"Nathalie, who killed herself. I remind you of her?"

"Yes. *Oui.* You do. I wrote the book for her."

Marie liked that very much.

"Your sister," she said, intrigued by the incestuous undertones of this statement. He had lost his sister, but in her stead, he had found Marie. Eventually, Benoît would come to understand that their lives were inextricably bound. Ellen might have been good for him at one point in his life, what he had needed, just as Marie had once needed jail, the freedom to rest and to heal. He might even miss her, but his wife was not what Benoît needed.

Marie kissed him again, this time gentle and slow.

She could hear Caitlin running past.

"I am a sea lion," Caitlin said, pushing the air down with her arms as she ran. She had grown used to Benoît and Marie kissing.

His sister. Marie reminded Benoît Doniel of his long lost sister. Marie was Virginie. She was the love of his life.

Benoît packed Caitlin's things. Her favorite toys. Her favorite clothes, her favorite books, her DVDs. Caitlin had many favorite things. Benoît also had his books. His CDs. His clothes. He packed four matching suitcases and Caitlin's stroller. Marie put together a carry-on bag with things they would need on the plane.

"Nice luggage," Marie noted, nodding at the four full suitcases.

"A wedding gift," Benoît said.

Marie's belongings still fit in the backpack she had arrived with, even with Ellen's red kimono and various other small objects: earrings, silver bangles, lavender bubble bath.

What they were doing was not illegal. Caitlin was Benoît's child. They all had passports. Marie was not sure if it had been her idea, running away, or Benoît's, or if it was her idea that she had implanted into his head.

"Paris," Benoît said.

His eyes lit up with a crazy, manic, frantic glee. "There is no city like it. No other place compares. Nathalie used to tell me I could not survive anywhere else. We are going to Paris."

Benoît checked his wallet.

"I don't have the tickets," he said. "The plane tickets. I don't have them."

He had ordered them on the phone.

"E-tickets," Marie said. "They'll be at the counter."

Marie was stunned by the déjà vu. The leaving fast, the ridiculous thrill of leaving everything behind. This time it was slightly more complicated. Marie was traveling with juice cups and diapers, organic string cheese. A child. A stroller. This must be a sign that Marie was growing up.

"We are going to Paris!" she said, picking Caitlin up and spinning her around, faster and faster, until she fell down on top of the bed, taking Caitlin with her.

"This will all end badly," Benoît said, closing the last suitcase, but he was grinning. Caitlin's silky-smooth hair was in Marie's mouth. Her nose was running. Marie wiped it with the bottom of her T-shirt. They would still watch TV together, and they would take baths and go for walks in the afternoon. But in Paris. There were beautiful gardens in Paris, walks along the Seine. There was delicious food to be eaten.

"It will, you know?" Benoît said.

"No," Marie said. "I don't know that."

Juan José had ended up dead, hanging from a bedsheet. She had last seen him at the courthouse; they had both been wearing prison uniforms. She was sent in one direction, he in the other, and that was the last time she had ever seen him: handcuffed, looking down at the ground.

She twirled a strand of Caitlin's hair in her finger. She touched the tip of Benoît's beaky nose. It was a nose that belonged in Paris.

"Maybe," she said. "It won't."

They took a taxi to the airport.

They had dinner at the McDonald's by the gate. Already, Ellen's rules had become irrelevant. Caitlin ate her first cheeseburger and was overjoyed.

"I like it!" she said, licking her lips. "I like it. I like it!"

Caitlin was equally pleased with her french fries.

She also liked the plastic action figure that came in the box, a figure from a new movie neither Marie nor Benoît recognized.

Benoît's cell phone first started to ring in the McDonald's.

"It's Ellen," Benoît said.

Marie nodded.

Benoît did not answer.

The phone rang again in the magazine shop, and then it

rang again in the boarding area, while Marie read to Caitlin, pretending not to feel anxious about Benoît, who was nervously pacing. He had lit a cigarette and been asked by a police officer to put it out.

"I'll talk to Mommy?" Caitlin asked, reaching for the cell phone.

"No," Marie said, "Mommy is still at work," and she kept on reading. "Look, Caitlin. The teddy bear is still missing. You turn the page for me, okay?" and Caitlin turned the page.

Benoît didn't answer the cell phone, but he checked the caller ID each time it rang, a fresh wave of distress clouding his features. Marie did not ask who was calling because she did not need to. The plane could not board fast enough. Why was he so surprised? What did he think would happen? That Ellen would come home from work and not notice that they were gone? That she would do nothing? *Oops, no family.* Of course she would be unhappy. Of course she would call. They had decided to leave, to go to France. That was the choice they had made together, in front of the sea lions. Benoît only had to turn off his cell phone, but he could not seem to do it.

It was not until they boarded, after the airline attendants asked that they fasten their seat belts and turn off their electronic devices, not until the plane began taxiing down the runway, that he listened to his messages.

Marie held Caitlin's hand as the plane took off.

"Loud," Caitlin said.

Marie agreed.

Outside the window was the Atlantic Ocean. Marie stared down at the massive body of water beneath them. Ellen's phone calls had not stopped the plane. They were in flight, on their way to Europe. Marie had never thought she would make it there. Everything that Marie could possibly want was hers. Messages on a cell phone could not touch her. Benoît put the phone away. He rearranged the airline blanket over Caitlin, who had fallen asleep, her blond hair matted down on her tiny, perfect face, a smear of ketchup on her cheek.

"She says she'll have you arrested for kidnapping. She says that this time you'll never get out of prison. She'll make sure you rot in jail for the rest of your life. She says she has called the police. There is a warrant for your arrest. She says that this is the biggest mistake that I have ever made and that I will regret it, but not to worry. She says she'll forgive me."

"She'll forgive you?"

"That's what she said."

A woman in the row behind them tapped Benoît on the shoulder with a sock-covered foot. It was a striped sock, dark blue and turquoise.

"*C'est toi, non?*" she said, her voice a playful whisper. "Benoît Doniel? *Oui*. Benoît Doniel. Benoît Doniel."

Marie watched as Benoît did not respond to this voice. He looked at Marie.

"*Je sais que c'est toi. Je le sais. Je le sais.*"

Marie watched as the unidentified foot kicked him again, this time with more force.

"She knows you," Marie said.

"*Merde*," Benoît said.

The woman with the striped socks got out of her seat and came over. She crouched in the aisle next to Benoît Doniel and put her hands on his face. She kissed both cheeks, and then she kissed him long and hard on his mouth.

"Who is that?" Caitlin asked.

Marie shook her head.

"She has long hair," Caitlin said.

The woman's blond hair went down to her waist. Marie suppressed the temptation to pull it. When the woman was done kissing Benoît, she put her head in his lap and started to cry.

"Benoît?" Marie said.

Benoît rubbed the top of the crying woman's head. He looked at Marie.

"This is Lili Gaudet," he said. "I have not seen her in a very long time."

Marie nodded.

The woman lifted her head, crouching still in the aisle, wiping the tears away from her eyes. They were unusual eyes; the lids came down as if she might be part Asian. Only then did she notice Marie.

"You have not heard of me?" she said.

Marie shook her head.

"Should I have heard of you?"

"I am an actress," she said.

"I've been in prison," Marie said.

Lili Gaudet blinked.

She said something to Benoît in French.

He shrugged his shoulders.

"It's okay," he said.

"You live in New York," she said. "I was just in New York. My film was at the Tribeca Film Festival. They ate hot dogs, the audience, watching my movie."

"How awful for you."

"You must have known I was in New York." She looked back at Benoît. "Read about me in the newspaper?"

Benoît blinked.

"I didn't know, Lili."

Marie did not like the way Benoît spoke her name. The intimacy with which he said it.

"Is this your wife?" Lili Gaudet asked Benoît. "I heard that you were married. And who is this? Is this your little girl?"

"I am a big girl," Caitlin said.

"*Excusez-moi*. Is this your big girl?"

"*Oui*. Caitlin. *Elle a presque trois ans*."

"*Ta petite fille*." The French actress beamed at Caitlin, more tears welling in her eyes. "I have looked for him," she said to Marie. "*Je l'ai cherché et cherché*. All these years. I have looked for him."

And then, she started to weep. She fell into the arms of the airline attendant who had been hovering right behind.

Benoît unbuckled his seat belt.

"What are you doing?" Marie said. "Don't."

But Benoît stood up from his seat. He tapped the airline attendant, who transferred the burden of the French actress into his arms.

"The lady is crying," Caitlin said, excited, pointing.

Even worse, there were tears in Benoît's eyes.

"I looked for him," the French actress said to Marie, speaking over Benoît's shoulder. "And I looked. For years, I looked. I called his *grand-mère*, but she would not tell me. He did not want to be found. *Mon coeur etait battu. Comprends?*"

But then she smiled.

The French actress had a spectacular smile. With her arms wrapped around Benoît, she projected a deranged happiness. She appeared almost retarded in her delight. Marie was appalled.

"I love this man," Lili told Marie. "I love Benoît Doniel. *Je suis très heureuse* to see him again. *Comprends?*"

She kissed both of Benoît's cheeks again. His hair hung in his eyes.

"I want Elmo," Caitlin said, grabbing Marie's arm.

"I don't know where he is, Caty Cat."

"I want Elmo."

Marie was glad to have a reason to interrupt the French actress's moment of rapture. "Do you know where it is, Benoît? Caitlin's Elmo. Did you pack it?"

"It's in one of the suitcases."

"I want Elmo," Caitlin said.

"It's checked, Caitlin," Marie said.

She took a stuffed rabbit from the bag.

"*Voilà*," Marie said.

Caitlin shook her head.

"No." Marie stroked the soft fur of the rabbit's floppy ears. She liked the rabbit.

"Who is talking to Daddy?" Caitlin said.

Marie turned to look. She did not know what word to use: bitch, cunt, French actress. Instead she shrugged her shoulders.

"I want a cheeseburger," Caitlin said, her voice rising. "I want Mommy. Where is Mommy?"

"Mommy is at work, Silly Bean," Marie said.

At home, Caitlin never asked for her mother. Ellen could work a fourteen-hour day and no one would miss her. Caitlin was always happy to be with Marie, happy to spend their days together. Sometimes, Caitlin was already asleep when Ellen came home from work.

"Do you want me to read to you?"

Marie, the efficient and capable babysitter, pulled out the book about a lost teddy bear from her bag beneath the seat and began to read to Caitlin, while Benoît remained in the aisle with his deranged French actress. Marie read to Caitlin as Benoît sat next to Lili Gaudet in the row behind them. While Caitlin turned the page, Marie craned her neck to get a glimpse of the French actress, talking to Benoît in rapid French, holding his hand.

He had left his wife, he had left his home. For her. For Marie. She had saved him from drudgery and dominion. But there he was, sitting with another woman, another woman who kissed him on the mouth, burst into tears, and talked of his grandmother. It was all wrong. The French actress was pretty enough; her hair was blond and long, she wore a black T-shirt that clung to her breasts, but her head was enormous compared to the rest of her body. Her dark eyes were almost ferretlike, darting. She was skinny, too skinny. She leaned her head against Benoît's shoulder.

Benoît looked at Marie through the crack in the seats, attempting to nod reassuringly, at the same moment the airline attendant brought over two glasses of champagne. Marie was not reassured. It was too soon for Marie to be angry with Benoît. Too early to begin with regrets and recriminations.

Marie did not believe in regret. It was not, for instance, her fault that Juan José had chosen to kill himself. She could not have known that would happen when he appeared at her doorstep. Marie looked away from Benoît, from his French actress. She could hear their glasses clink together, the French actress laughing, a sound that was just as repellent as the French actress's crying outburst. Marie picked up Caitlin's hand and pretended to bite it.

"I am eating your hand," Marie said. "I am eating it up. Yummy, yummy hands."

Caitlin had such perfect little hands, tiny chubby fingers.

"Don't," Caitlin said, laughing. "Don't. Stop. Don't."

"Well," Marie said. "What do we do?"

"Let's watch the TV," Caitlin said.

Marie nodded, reassured. Caitlin still knew how to behave. Marie put the headset on Caitlin's little head; she found French cartoons playing on the built-in screen on the seat in front of them. A black cat said: "Ooh la la."

"Ooh la la la la," Caitlin said. "La la la."

"Ooh ooh ooh," Marie said.

"La la la."

It was not necessary to speak French to enjoy the French cartoon about the black cat. Caitlin did not want her mommy; she had only needed to establish her mother's location. Elmo was in the suitcase. Mommy was at the office. Caitlin didn't even need Benoît. Only Marie. Marie found a bag of cheddar cheese goldfish crackers she'd packed in the carry-on bag, and they ate them happily, watching the television. Marie tried not to think longingly of the flat-screen TV in Ellen's living room, the comfortable leather couch where she had watched so many bad TV movies. The routine she and Caitlin had painstakingly perfected, the life Marie had left behind.

Marie had been happy in Ellen's home.

The French actress looked fragile. She looked like she relied on men, needed a man to help her breathe. Any second now, she'd lower her head, currently on Benoît's shoulder, down to his lap.

"Don't," she said to Caitlin, "be like that. Ever."

After they landed, Benoît and the French actress talked all the way through the airport and then through customs, where Marie and Caitlin had to stand in a separate line for foreigners. The French actress and Benoît kept on talking at the baggage claim while Marie scrambled for all of the ridiculous bags. They came in, one by one: the four suitcases, then the stroller, and, finally, Marie's backpack.

"That's everything," Marie told Benoît.

Marie loaded the bags onto a cart while Benoît talked to the French actress.

"Push this," she told Benoît, and he did.

Marie held Caitlin's hand. She nodded to the French actress, but that was all. The flight was over and it was time to say good-bye. But when the moment arrived, when Benoît and Marie and Caitlin were supposed to get into a French taxicab and start their life together in Paris, France, Marie found themselves still attached to Lili Gaudet, who ushered them out of the airport and toward a black car that was waiting.

"You will stay with me," she explained to Marie. "I have plenty of room. You'll be very comfortable. I have many rooms." She looked at Caitlin. "I have toys for you. Beautiful dolls."

Marie looked at Benoît. She had never thought to ask him where they would go once they were in Paris. She had thought they would talk about this, their plans, on the airplane, but instead he had gone off with the French actress. Marie assumed he had some sort of plan. It was his country.

"This is good," Benoît assured Marie. "It's lucky that we found Lili. Ellen will not be able to find us in her apartment."

"*Ta femme?*" Lili asked. "Ellen?"

"Mommy?" Caitlin said. "Where is Mommy?"

Marie wished Caitlin would stop talking about Ellen.

"He did not invite me to the wedding," Lili said. Lili was gripping the bottom of Benoît's sweater, like a child.

"I was in prison," Marie said.

Lili looked confused, but she didn't respond. Marie understood what she was doing. The French actress would treat Marie as if she was the babysitter. The servant. As if she did not exist.

"She already knows we are in France," Benoît told Marie.

"How?" Marie asked. "How does she know?"

"The credit card. The plane tickets."

Marie nodded. They had thought nothing through. Eluding Ellen would be harder than the police. Caitlin was off her nap schedule. There would be jet lag to contend with.

"You haven't talked to Ellen?" Marie said. "Have you?"

Marie did not see how he could have, since he had spent every single second with the French actress, but she also couldn't be sure.

Benoît shook his head. "Just the messages."

"Wishing me a life in prison."

"If I pay for a hotel on her credit card, she will know where to look."

"You don't have a credit card in your own name?"

"Marie," he said, irritated.

"I live in the best *arrondissement* in Paris," the French actress said, speaking loudly as if that would improve her English. "You can walk everywhere. The best restaurants, the nicest gardens, the best museums. Shopping. Do you know Paris?" Lili Gaudet did not wait for Marie's answer. "It is a beautiful city. The most beautiful in the world. I used to tell Benoît I could not imagine him anywhere else."

"That's what his sister told him," Marie said.

Benoît had begun to load all the luggage into the trunk of the black car, helping the driver, which made it impossible for him to contribute to the conversation and also made the decision to go to Lili Gaudet's apartment final. Four bags and a stroller.

"Car seat," Caitlin said, when Marie tried to put her in the car.

They'd packed everything else, but not the car seat.

Marie never had to worry about these details before. Caitlin had not demanded a car seat the day before, when they took a taxi to the zoo. Marie looked at Lili Gaudet, and her mind flashed back to the prison, the intense heat of the laundry room, the simple monotony of folding clothes. There were no serious mistakes to make in prison. There was only work to do, sheets and towels and uniforms to clean, and then more laundry, a never-ending supply, until her body ached with exhaustion. Marie closed her eyes, just for a second, and she breathed in deep. The Paris air was redolent with exhaust fumes.

"A seat belt is good, too," Marie told Caitlin.

"No," Caitlin said. "Car seat."

"You'll be fine, Kit Kat. I'll just strap you in. You'll see."

"She misses her mother, no?" Lili said.

Marie understood that Lili was trying to undercut Marie's authority. They were not and would never be friends. Marie went to the trunk, where Benoît was still busy with the bags, and she picked a suitcase at random. She opened it and found Caitlin's Elmo.

"*C'est* Elmo," Lili said. "We have him here, too, in France."

Marie handed the red stuffed doll to Caitlin.

"Elmo," Caitlin said, hugging the red doll to her chest. Marie buckled Caitlin's seat belt and sat down next to Caitlin in the backseat, her knees bent to her chest, her feet up on the bump, and Lili sat down next to her. She was wearing a flowery perfume that Marie did not like.

"You will love my apartment," she said.

Benoît was in front, next to the driver. Marie rolled down the window on Lili's side, and then they were off.

This is Paris, Marie thought, staring at the congested highway. She closed her eyes, and she was transported back, again, to the prison laundry, standing on the opposite end of a bedsheet from Ruby Hart, Ruby with her broad cheeks, her thin lips, her orange uniform; Ruby taking hold of the end of the sheet as Marie brought the other end to her, halving the sheet, and taking the other end from Marie's hand, and then they folded it in half again, and then again, until it was a small rectangle, and Ruby would fold one last time while Marie went to the stack to get the next sheet, for them to begin again. Sheet after sheet after sheet.

The walls of Lili Gaudet's apartment were lined with books.
Apparently, she was a smart actress. Marie looked for a copy of
Virginie at Sea and she found it, a French edition she had never
seen before, next to a collection of poetry by Nathalie Doniel.

Marie took the slim paperback from the shelf. She glanced
through it quickly; the poems were written in French. Marie
turned to the back page for the author photo and she blinked.
She wondered, for a moment, if she was looking at a picture
of herself. It was true. Marie looked like Benoît Doniel's dead
sister.

Still holding the poems, Marie reached for *Virginie at
Sea*. Unlike Marie's edition, which had a black-and-white
drawing of a girl and a sea lion on the cover, Lili's book had
a photograph of a desolate beach, nothing more. The title in
small black letters was different, too. *Virginie à la mer*. Marie
opened the book, surprised again, and somehow disturbed, to
see that this, too, was written in French.

On the shelf was also a framed photo, a black-and-white print of Lili Gaudet and Benoît and Nathalie, the dead sister who was not yet dead. It had been taken when they were teenagers. The three of them were all dressed alike in blue jeans and white button-down shirts, their expressions ridiculously serious, staring into the camera.

Marie could not look away.

Benoît had never before mentioned the French actress, but they had a history, tied up with the dead sister, who Benoît seemed to idolize in death the way Marie remembered Juan José. Marie was stunned by her resemblance to the dead sister. The thick dark hair and the dark eyes. Even the amount of space between their dark eyes. The petulant stare. The substantial chest. Nathalie's arms were crossed, as if to cover her cleavage. Marie used to do that, too, when she was a teenager. Marie was glad to be thirty years old and in command of her chest.

Marie felt more secure, knowing how much she looked like Nathalie. This man, this French writer, he was not an accident. He was not a passing fancy, a way to get back at Ellen for the inequities of her childhood. Marie was not just another woman in a long list of women. She was a reincarnation of Benoît's dead sister. They were meant for each other. "Destiny," that was the word that came into Marie's mind.

Marie worried she was neglecting Caitlin, but she could hear Benoît and Lili, talking, getting settled into the apartment, taking Caitlin with them on their tour; Marie could hear drinks being poured, the infernal cheeks being kissed again, that horrible sound. She could not stop staring at the photo. At the much younger Benoît. Years younger than even his author photo. Decidedly less handsome. Awkward. His hair was short, too short. He wore a narrow necktie, a fitted jacket, cuff links. He wore a dangling earring in his right ear. His face was wide open, without secrets. He had no American wife. No dead sister. No knowledge of what was to come.

Lili walked over to Marie. She took the books out of Marie's hands and returned them to the shelf. "I love that photo," she said. "I also loved Nathalie. Very much. She was my best friend. Both of them, Nathalie and Benoît. My best friends in the whole world, though Benoît, he was more than that. *Comprends?* He was my very first. You don't forget your first love. Or love again like that. *Comprends?*"

Marie stared at Lili, keeping her face blank. She did not want to be hearing this information. It was inappropriate.

"I wanted to kill him," Lili pointed at Benoît, "when he left for America. He just disappeared. Gone. No good-bye. His grandmother tells me that he has married an American girl, but won't give me his address, his telephone number. I begged her but she would not. She never liked me. First I lose Nathalie and then him."

She smiled at Marie, that insane, enormous, deranged toothy smile. Since entering the apartment, she had somehow lost the clingy black T-shirt and was down to a black camisole. "Now he is back."

She gestured toward Benoît, who stood hesitant in the doorway; he crouched down to Caitlin's level, holding her hand.

Lili turned back to Marie, waiting for her to respond. Marie had nothing to say. She returned Lili's gaze, perfectly prepared to outlast her.

"I don't know what to think of this," Lili said. "I am in, how do you say, shock."

Marie searched for Benoît's eyes, but he did not rescue her from his French actress. Instead, he led Caitlin to the bathroom and closed the door. Marie hoped he would change Caitlin's diaper. Marie supposed she couldn't fault Benoît for that. She would need help with Caitlin. Soon Caitlin was supposed to start potty training. Ellen had recently informed Marie that this next developmental stage was imminent; she had given Marie all sorts of child development books to read. Marie had never bothered, because Caitlin hadn't been her baby. Marie stared at the closed door of the bathroom, willing them to come back.

Lili snapped her fingers.

"It's amazing, no? That we are all on the same airplane. This is, how do you say, fate? Yes, fate. He has a child. She must look like the wife? Benoît's wife. *Elle est très jolie?*"

Marie shook her head.

"She looks like herself. Like Caitlin."

"Remind me to speak always in English," Lili said. "Okay? You remind me. *Comprends?* You understand?"

"I understand."

"Who are you?" Lili asked. "If you are not the wife? Are you the girlfriend?"

"Yes," Marie said.

"*Vraiment?* For how long?" Lili asked.

Marie did not answer.

"For how long have you been his girlfriend?"

Again, Marie did not answer.

"You look like his sister," Lili said.

Marie nodded.

"That must be what he sees in you."

Marie would not answer that, either.

"But you are not as beautiful as Nathalie. He might be confused. They did not have parents, you know?"

Somehow, Marie did not know this. But it was a lie, anyway, what the French actress was telling her. Everyone had parents. They might die or disappoint you, but you could not be born without them.

"This whole day," Lili said, "has been a shock. If I seem rude. *Comprends?*"

"I understand," Marie said. "I am his girlfriend. Do you understand?"

The word sounded inadequate next to Lili Gaudet's black camisole. Not that the French actress had any cleavage. What she had, though, was history. He had returned her kiss on the airplane. Marie had seen that.

Benoît and Caitlin returned from the bathroom. Caitlin ran over to Marie and wrapped herself around her leg.

"I can't believe you didn't come see me at the festival," Lili said to Benoît. "I was written about in the newspapers. I not only acted, I wrote the screenplay. The Americans, they are horrible, the audiences. They walked out in the middle. They ate hot dogs. You could have called me, Benoît. All this time, you could have called me. I have not moved. My telephone number has not changed."

Benoît shrugged.

"I had to get away," he said.

It had never once occurred to Marie that Benoît Doniel knew other people in the world outside of herself and Caitlin.

"Have you seen my movies?" Lili asked him.

Benoît shrugged again. "Oh, Lili."

"You haven't seen any of my movies? I have been in many movies. I always thought, Benoît, Benoît will see me in this film, and he will call me."

"I haven't seen them."

"Have you?" she asked Marie.

"I think I told you. I have been in jail," Marie said. "They didn't show French films."

"They do have books," Benoît quipped.

Marie looked at Benoît and smiled.

"I am disgusted by you," Lili said to Benoît. "*Comprends?*"

Benoît nodded. He sat down on Lili's sofa, a leather sofa much like Ellen's. He lit a cigarette and put his feet on the coffee table. This was a room he seemed to know and know well. He was unnervingly comfortable.

"You have read his book?" Lili asked Marie.

Again, Marie did not answer Lili's question. She did not care if she seemed stupid. She refused to compete. She would not acknowledge this competition. She had already won. Ellen had come home from work to an empty apartment.

"She did," Benoît said. "She read it in the American prison. I don't want to talk about my book."

"Did you love it?" the French actress said. "Why were you in jail? How long have you been Benoît's girlfriend? Do you really believe he loves you? Do you? He only loves himself. He is the most selfish bastard on the planet. He doesn't see my movies. I have won two César Awards since he left me. I am famous. He does not love you."

Marie looked at Benoît.

He needed to control his French actress.

"I'm hungry," Caitlin said.

They left their unpacked bags in Lili Gaudet's apartment in
the best neighborhood in Paris and went to the restaurant
down the block, where Marie ordered the first thing she recognized on the menu, the steak frites, which she loved. Marie
drank the delicious red wine Benoît ordered and she ate her
steak, charred on the outside, red on the inside, drizzled with
a thick pepper sauce, and she marveled at herself, sitting in a
restaurant in France, eating delicious steak.

Ruby Hart was still in prison. Juan José was still dead.
Marie's mother was simmering in the same old, ugly house
she'd lived in for the past thirty years. Marie was in Paris. The
French bread was just as good as Benoît Doniel had promised
it would be.

At the restaurant, the French actress resumed talking in
French, talking talking talking, but Marie did not feel jealous.
In fact, she felt relieved. Marie did not want to talk. She did
not want to explain herself. She did not want to understand

what had once happened between Lili and Benoît or know what they were saying to each other. She did not want to know. She wanted to eat. She wanted Caitlin to eat. In a strange way, with the horrible French actress commanding all of Benoît's attention, Marie was alone again with Caitlin. They had been happy together, before Benoît.

"Hi Caitlin," Marie said.

"Hi Marie," Caitlin said.

"Hi Kit Kat," Marie said.

"Hi Marie," Caitlin said.

"Everyone speaks French in France," she told Caitlin.

Caitlin reached for a french fry off of Marie's plate.

"This is called a *frite* in France," Marie said.

"*Frite,*" Caitlin echoed.

She ate it and then she reached for another.

Marie drank her wine. Caitlin drank her milk. Instead of chocolate pudding for dessert, they ordered the chocolate mousse.

"This," Marie said, "tastes better."

She enjoyed her dinner, despite the fact that Benoît Doniel had abandoned them. The French actress had taken him, brought him over to the bar, introduced him to the bartender and a woman with short hair wearing a red blouse and blue jeans. Marie watched Benoît kiss the cheeks of these people.

"Daddy is over there." Caitlin pointed.

Marie nodded.

"Mommy is at work."

"Your Mommy works hard," Marie said. She looked into the almost empty bowl of chocolate mousse and ate the last spoonful.

When the waiter returned, Marie ordered a whiskey

and another chocolate mousse. She asked for these things in English and the waiter understood.

When the bill came, Lili Gaudet paid.

"I am very rich," she told Marie, leaning over to get her wallet out of her purse, flashing the thin straps of her black camisole beneath a shapeless gray sweater.

Back at her apartment, while Marie got Caitlin ready for bed, the French actress continued to talk. She had Benoît Doniel cornered on the edge of the leather couch, with no choice but to listen, her skinny arms waving wildly. At some point, Marie realized she had reverted back to crying. She was, clearly, hysterical, and she was also waiting for Benoît to react. Marie wondered if Lili Gaudet might suffer from some sort of acute mental condition.

The French actress could enter a mental hospital, and they could live happily in her big apartment in the best neighborhood in Paris.

Marie recognized the fact that Benoît might need saving, but she had just saved him from his wife. His wife. Ellen Kendall. That had required heroic effort. They had been standing there, defeated, at the sea lion tank, and he had tried to find a way to say good-bye to Marie. Instead, they were together. In France.

She would rescue Benoît again, later. Before that, Marie would give Caitlin a bath. It was the same routine, in New York or in Paris. They took the bath together, Marie and Caitlin. They were more than fine on their own. Caitlin, at least, seemed fine.

"Bubbles," she said.

Benoît had remembered Caitlin's plastic ducks. Marie found them in the third suitcase. She took Ellen's lavender

bubble bath from her backpack. She then located a good bottle
of Irish whiskey in the French actress's kitchen and poured
herself a glass. It had been a long, long day.

Caitlin was too tired to play with her ducks.

Marie would have to rouse herself, make sure to actually
wash Caitlin before they got out. She lay back in the bathtub
with her drink. She would not fall asleep; she would not pass
out.

"I'll wash your hair," Marie said. "What do you say?"

Caitlin nodded her head.

Marie blinked, taking in the bathroom, remembering
again where she was. In Paris. On the run. Not in a hotel, but
the apartment of Benoît's French actress. The off-white rect-
angular bathtub was tiny, basic—much too small for Benoît
to join them. The bathroom itself was also simple, unexceptional. Lili Gaudet couldn't have been much of a movie star.

They were quiet in bed, having sex in France in the French actress's apartment. Because Benoît did not want Lili Gaudet to hear them.

"Why have sex at all?" Marie said.

But she didn't mean it. Silent sex was exciting in its own way. They were quieter than they had ever been; it had been safe before, Ellen had always been at work. The danger, then, had been in the cleaning; keeping the sheets fresh, not leaving any hairs in untoward places.

Benoît and Marie had never had sex at night, never in the dark, and this was different for Marie, not being able to see Benoît's body, his face, but still to know him, to taste him, to recognize his touch. His mouth, teeth, on her breast, sucking. Marie was silent, silently reclaiming Benoît Doniel from the French actress.

Sex. It reminded Marie, who was drunk and tired and angry, appalled by this ferretlike French actress in their life, why she was with Benoît. Reminded her that she was hope-lessly in love. Marie was glad she had not fallen asleep after her bath. Silently, she pushed him in deeper and harder. In those six years of prison, there had been no sex. Every time she was with Benoît, Marie felt grateful. Alive. She wanted more.

She could be quiet.

Nothing was lost.

They had run away together.

They still had this passion.

In the morning, when they awoke, there would be fresh croissants, made in Paris.

"I love you," Marie said.

It felt especially generous to say these words, given the way the day had gone. It was the first time that she ever told Benoît that she loved him, and Benoît returned Marie's dec-laration with a soft murmur, delivered into the bony flesh of her shoulder. "*Moi aussi*," Marie heard him say, meaningless words, more so because they were spoken in French, but Marie was appeased. She believed in the promise of the coming day. The certainty of breakfast.

Marie had forgotten how it felt, to fall asleep with another person. Benoît was smaller than Marie. She held him tight, spooning her body around his.

Marie woke up and saw Lili Gaudet sitting on a black leather beanbag chair in the corner of the guest bedroom, watching them. She was wearing a sheer black nightgown that barely covered her thighs.

"You have nice breasts," she told Marie.

Benoît lay on his side, sleeping. Marie reached for the sheet, covering their nakedness.

"They are much bigger than mine," the French actress said.

"Leave," Marie said.

"Are they real? Your breasts?"

Marie did not answer.

Lili chewed on a strand of long blond hair.

"Thank you for bringing him back to me," she said. "Really, I am grateful. He's been gone for too long. I have been waiting for him to come back. I knew someday he would come back. I will give you money. You can travel. Or go home to your America."

"And my hot dogs."

"I don't understand."

"Hot dogs," Marie said. "Americans like hot dogs."

"*Dégoûtant*," Lili Gaudet said. "I will give you money. You can go home. Or you can stay in Paris. Why not? It is a big city. It does not matter to me where you go. I am a very successful actress. I will help you. He belongs to me. He knows that. You know that. *Comprends?*"

Marie lowered the sheet to show off her large, real breasts.

"You know it won't last," the French actress said. "He will have sex with anyone. He was always like this. Nathalie did not want him to meet any of her friends. He did not care how it made her feel. He'll fuck anything. *Comprends?* Ask him. Wake him up. Wake him up."

Marie leaned over, gently shaking Benoît Doniel's shoulder. Benoît tried to kiss her, put his hands in her hair, and Marie let him pull her down. She wanted the French actress to watch, to let the French actress know what happened between them in bed.

"*Arrête*," the French actress said.

This stopped Benoît.

"She is in our room," Marie whispered.

"My room," Lili said. "My apartment, my room."

"Lili?" Benoît broke away from Marie, sitting up in the bed.

"Three years," Lili said, addressing Benoît and only Benoît, but speaking slowly and deliberately in English, for Marie's sake. "Three years you have been gone. Not a word. You have another woman's baby."

"I had to leave," he said. "I didn't have to explain it to you. I owed you nothing."

"You did owe me," she said. "You made promises to me."

"My sister died." Benoît's voice was angry. "She killed herself. She hanged herself in your summer house. You were there. You discovered her body."

"Every night and every day, that summer, you fucked me."

"You misunderstood, Lili," he said. "We were crazy. With grief. That's all it was. I had to get away. You are fine. You are a big star. You knew you would be."

With that, Lili Gaudet started again, speaking in rapid French. Marie heard that one same word at the end of almost every sentence, repeatedly. *Comprends? Comprends? Comprends?* Because apparently, Benoît did not. He did not want to give her whatever it was that she required. The French actress waved her arms, she chewed on her hair, and then she came over to the bed, she pulled the sheet off of Marie and called her a name. Marie did not know the word, but she understood what it meant: whore, slut, something hateful. Marie thought that women didn't get to call other women whores or sluts anymore. And then she noticed that the French actress was staring again at Marie's breasts, and when Marie looked down, she could see the spot where Benoît had sunk his teeth. He had bitten hard, as if he had literally tried to consume her.

Benoît got out of the bed, naked, and he went for Lili before she could get to Marie. Marie was grateful. The fingernails of the French actress were long, her rodentlike eyes crazed. Benoît grabbed Lili Gaudet by the shoulders and tried to force her to the door. A strap from her nightgown fell off her shoulder, revealing a breast. Her breasts were small, much smaller than Marie's, but they were perfectly formed, and Marie noticed, while Benoît tried to force the French actress away from the bed, that his dangling penis had become aroused, and Lili Gaudet was crying, again, as she started to punch Benoît with her fists. "*Je te déteste*," she repeated, striking wildly.

Marie felt more tired than she had ever remembered being. More tired than the day Ellen's mother explained that she could not pay for her college education, but offered her a small sum for textbooks. More tired than the day she was released from prison and realized that there was no one to pick her up. Marie sat upright in the bed and watched them: the French insanity show. She did not defend what was hers.

Served her right.

That was what her mother would say. She said that every time Marie got into trouble: for shoplifting a lipstick at the mall, for getting caught cheating on an algebra test, for going to prison for abetting a violent felon.

Served her right. Her mother's words.

Her mother would be ashamed if she knew what Marie had done to Ellen's marriage. Her mother had taken Ellen's side when it had all come out about Harry Alford. She'd think Marie was getting exactly what she deserved, witnessing the sick and twisted dance of Marie's adulterous lover and his insane French actress.

"*Comprends?*" the French actress screamed. She punched Benoît in the chest. Over and over. With every *comprends*.

The ridiculous hair that Marie loved swooped down into Benoît Doniel's eyes, but Marie couldn't miss the change that had come over him; at a certain point, Benoît had stopped defending himself against Lili Gaudet's crazed punches. He had stopped trying to push her to the door.

Marie watched as he broke down and did the absolute

worst possible thing that he could do. Marie watched while Benoît kissed Lili Gaudet, his hands in the French actress's long, tangled blond hair, his tongue in her mouth. Marie even understood, a little, the pull of nostalgia. To get a second chance. To slip back into your past, to be the person that you once were. To return to your youth, your lost love. Marie had never thought that Benoît Doniel would take the place of Juan José, but he had left his wife for her. He had left the safety and comfort of his wife and taken his child and traveled across an ocean. He had done all of this for Marie, and here he was, embracing this French actress right in front of her, as she sat naked on the bed where he had just fucked her, and if Marie believed in fate, which she seemed to, then there seemed to be something fated about this, too. Fate had given Marie Benoît Doniel, and now fate was taking him away.

Benoît Doniel was kissing Lili Gaudet in front of Marie. Lili was still crying, pressing herself against him, stroking his unmistakably erect penis with one hand, holding him close with the other. Marie listened to the French actress moan with pleasure. And Marie, she just watched, paralyzed on the bed that her lover and the reprehensible French actress would soon need, before she decided, finally, that this was more than she could take. Struggling to stand on legs that would not bend, Marie dragged herself out of the bed.

She wrapped herself in the sheet, a beautiful pale lavender sheet with small pink flowers, maybe the nicest sheet Marie had ever slept on, and she left the bedroom, walking carefully around Benoît Doniel and his French actress, hoping that he would cease in this madness when she passed by. But he didn't, and Marie made it safely into the living room, where earlier she had tucked Caitlin into a makeshift crib, couch pillows lined up on the floor next to the couch, a row upright, blocking her in. Beautiful, sweet Caitlin, asleep on the living-room floor, thumb in her mouth.

"Paris," Marie said to Caitlin, staring at the cobblestone street that lay ahead of them. There were expensive-looking shops lining both sides of the street. There was a lingerie store, a bakery. A bar. The restaurant where they had eaten steak frites. A bookstore. There were beautiful people, walking dogs, in stylish clothes.

Marie also found a bank, though she was too early. Marie did, at least, have money. She had four weeks' babysitting salary, practically untouched, and the five one-hundred-dollar bills, the guilt money Ellen had handed over the last time they saw each other. Marie would change these dollars to euros. She had money; she and Caitlin would be able to last awhile.

"We are in Paris," Marie said again. "Those birds you hear singing are French birds."

"French birds," Caitlin said.

"You got it," Marie said. "Exactly. French birds. They don't understand English. Not even a little bit."

Caitlin looked at Marie, not sure how to respond.

"And over there," Marie said, pointing to a little white poodle on a blue leash, "is a French dog."

"Doggie!"

Caitlin clapped her hands. The Frenchwoman walking the dog kindly allowed Caitlin to pet her dog. Caitlin was always happy, petting someone else's dog. Marie watched as the poodle licked Caitlin's face. Caitlin squealed. The woman smiled at Marie and Marie smiled at the Frenchwoman. Marie realized she would do fine on her own in France. French people did not look at her and think *kidnapper*.

Benoît Doniel could have his French actress. If that's what he wanted. It was unthinkable, really, that that was what he wanted, who he wanted, but Marie would be okay with that. She would revise her opinion of him. She had believed that she truly loved him, but that might have only ever been an idea. A concept. A crush on the author of *Virginie at Sea*. She did not need him, no, she had used him to get to France, a place she had never been before. She would go to the top of the Eiffel Tower. She would take Caitlin.

"We need breakfast," Marie said. "Are you hungry?"

Caitlin shook her head.

"I am hungry," Marie said.

"The doggie licked me," Caitlin said, smiling.

"I want to eat the best croissant in France," Marie said. "That's what I want."

They started to walk. They turned the corner onto another cobblestone street without shops, but lined with old and beautiful buildings, one after the other, flowers planted in beds of grass lining the sidewalks. Marie had no idea where they were. She could see the Eiffel Tower, but could not tell if it was near or far. Where were the museums the French actress had promised, or those famous gardens? Marie only knew that they were getting farther away from the French actress's apartment. She wondered how late Benoît would sleep, if he had managed to sleep, after he'd finished fucking his French actress. Maybe he had heard them leaving the apartment and he was racing to find them after waking up and discovering them gone.

With every step farther from the French actress's apartment, Marie felt a return to her better self. The Marie who did not care, who did not worry. Who took everything that was offered to her. Who did not look back. Caitlin was not unhappy. They started to walk as if it were any old day, as if New York was Paris and nothing had changed. They heard people speaking other languages in New York all the time. They walked one block and then another, turned right, and then right again; the view changed, the name of the street changed, and Marie found an outdoor market and a bubbling fountain. In the center of the square, near the market, French children were playing in the water. Dancing and splashing.

"I want to," Caitlin said, bending down to take off her shoes.

"Soon," Marie said. "First breakfast."

She was surprised by the adult tone of her voice. She was the responsible one, the one who told Caitlin what to do. Because she knew, by now, what Caitlin needed. Or maybe it was just that Marie was hungry. In need of coffee.

Marie found them a café out on the square, and she was able to order coffee, a croissant. She asked for everything in English. In France. This pleased Marie enormously.

"With milk?" the waitress asked, also in English. Because, of course, they spoke English in France. It was not much different from Mexico.

"Yes," Marie said. "In a bowl. Please."

"The milk in a bowl?"

"The coffee."

Marie also ordered milk for Caitlin. In a glass. And another croissant. And fruit. A fruit salad. Marie asked for everything in English and it was all delivered, along with three different kinds of jams she had not asked for and a chocolate hazelnut spread.

Marie dipped her croissant into the bowl of coffee the way she had watched Benoît Doniel dunk his food into his coffee. This made Marie happy, though she would have rather shared the experience of her first coffee and croissant with Benoît. She was not happy to have left him. They had not lasted a day together. Not a single day. But Marie did not see what else there was for her to have done. She could still picture him, his hands in the French actress's hair, his penis erect. Caitlin dipped her fingers into the pots of jam and then licked them clean.

"We like it in France?" Marie said. "*Oui?*"

Caitlin shook her head.

"No," she said. And then she changed her mind. "Weeee," she said.

She liked the jam, and Marie let her keep on eating it with her fingers. Caitlin had no interest in her croissant, but she drank her milk. She had gotten good with a glass, no longer needed a sippy cup. She was growing up. In the month they'd been together, Caitlin had gotten bigger, her hair longer. She grinned at Marie. There was jam in her hair. On her nose. On her yellow flowered T-shirt.

"Look at you, Caty Bean."

Marie did not really believe that she had walked out on
Benoît Doniel, taking his daughter with her. Benoît could take
Caitlin from his wife, but Marie had no right to take the girl
from her father. That was illegal; it had to be. But Marie could
not fathom leaving the French actress's apartment without
Caitlin. She could not imagine her life without Caitlin.

The croissant, at least, was delicious. Lighter and flakier
than any croissant she had ever had. It tasted like butter. And
the coffee, it was also delicious. When the waitress came back
around again, Marie ordered another.

"Do you want to eat your fruit?" she asked Caitlin.

Caitlin didn't.

Marie gladly ate Caitlin's fruit. The strawberries were
smaller in France. Marie thought she should tell Caitlin what
she was missing, insist that she should try the strawberries,
but instead Marie ate them, every last one. She could not help
herself. She had never tasted strawberries like these. They
made her happy.

"Hi Caitlin," Marie said, smiling at the little girl, fingers
still in the jam.

"Hi Marie."

"Hi Caty Bean."

"Hi Marie."

After breakfast, they would have to do something, go
somewhere. Caitlin's things, the bags and bags of favorite
things Benoît had feverishly packed, were still in Lili Gaudet's apartment. Marie had grabbed only Caitlin's travel bag,
Caitlin, and her own backpack, leaving everything else behind.
She wished she had taken Caitlin's stroller. A couple of stuffed
animals. The Elmo doll. Caitlin's father.

"What do you want to do next?" Marie said.

"I want to see sea lions," Caitlin said.

Marie nodded. It was the right thing to do, symbolic. Whenever Marie required wisdom, she could count on Caitlin.

"How did you get so smart?" Marie asked her.

Caitlin grinned.

"We'll go to the zoo," Marie said. There had to be a zoo in Paris.

"Where is Mommy?" Caitlin asked.

"Mommy?" Marie only missed a beat. "Mommy is at the office."

"Look at my fingers," Caitlin said.

They were sticky with jam. She smeared jam on Marie's bare arm. "Red," Caitlin said.

Marie licked the jam off her arm. She licked Caitlin's nose. Caitlin seemed to be satisfied with Marie's answer. It was the same as in the airport. Caitlin did not miss her mother; she just needed to know her whereabouts.

"Your daddy is busy, too," Marie said. "He is with the French actress."

"There," Caitlin said. "There is Daddy."

Caitlin pointed, and there, in fact, was Benoît Doniel. His face was bright red, covered in a glossy sheen of sweat. His button-down shirt was unbuttoned and untucked. He doubled over once he reached them, hands on his thighs, catching his breath. His legs shook violently. He opened his mouth to speak but couldn't.

"Of course," he said, finally. "Of course. Of course. *Bien sûr.* You are having breakfast. No need to worry."

Caitlin put her finger back into the pot of jam and offered it to Benoît. Benoît shook his head. He was staring at Marie.

Marie couldn't recognize the expression on his face. Love? Fear? Rage? She was inclined to think it was the latter, though she had never seen Benoît Doniel angry before. She did know what he looked like aroused by another woman.

"Good morning," he said to Marie. "You have already eaten. That's good. Very good. She went out for breakfast. That's all. That's okay. Sensible. You were hungry."

"No," Marie said. "I left."

Benoît looked around for the waitress.

"I left you," Marie said. "Then we decided on breakfast."

"We saw French birds," Caitlin said. "I pet a dog. This is good." She dipped her fingers back into the jam.

"Don't do that," Benoît said, taking Caitlin's hands out of the pot. "Why do you let her do that?"

It was the first time Benoît had ever criticized Marie for the way that she looked after Caitlin. Marie did not appreciate Benoît's look of contempt. For the first time, he reminded her of Ellen. He had chosen to marry that woman. Why? Because she drank Diet Coke? Because she paid his bills? Was she even any good in bed? Marie doubted it. She reached for Caitlin's croissant and took a bite.

Benoît ordered his breakfast in French, which seemed like just one more betrayal. But there they were, together, at a café in Paris, France, the way it was supposed to be. Standing in front of the sea lion tank, Marie had believed in them, in their future. She had thought everything was possible. They had been happy in New York, eating macaroni and cheese, taking walks to the park, taking baths in the afternoon. That had been real. Marie had been in love before and she recognized what it felt like.

"I know somewhere else we can stay," Benoît said. "With my grandmother."

"Good," Marie said.

She needed some place to stay. Hotels in Paris would use up her meager savings in a matter of days. Marie was glad that Benoît Doniel had found them when he did. He could also pay for breakfast.

"I'm sorry, Marie," Benoît said. "I beg you to forgive me."

"I don't want to hear that."

"We have a complicated history," Benoît said. "Lili *et moi*."

The waitress came with Benoît's coffee. He had gotten an espresso, not coffee in a bowl.

"I don't want to know about her."

"But you want to know about me. I am telling you about myself. Lili is practically a sister to me."

"You have sex with all of your sisters?" Marie immediately regretted saying that. She didn't want to engage him in this conversation. Did not want to be something as trivial as jealous. He could have this fight, later, with Ellen. "Don't answer that. I don't want to know."

"I want to tell you."

Marie shook her head.

"Tell me," Caitlin said. "Tell me, Daddy. Tell me."

Caitlin could not walk fast enough for Benoît. He kept trying to hurry her along. Caitlin stopped at every new thing that she saw, and they were passing through an enormous flea market; there were many things to see. They got stuck at the fish tanks, rows and rows of colored fish. Marie would not have expected it. Fish for sale on the streets of Paris. Benoît bought Caitlin an orange goldfish in a small glass bowl.

"I like it," Caitlin said.

"You'll have to carry that now," Marie told Benoît.

She was disturbed by the tone of her voice. Like an angry mother. Like a wife. She understood that she was mad at Benoît, but despite herself, she couldn't maintain a sense of righteous anger. The market fascinated her: live fish and also dead fish for consumption; all sorts of produce and cheese, meats, and then, farther down the street, stall after stall of books, used books, new books, art books, postcards, prints. All of this across the street from the Seine.

It was springtime, and Marie was in Paris, and she could not help it, she felt excited. She wanted to go everywhere, see everything, even though she didn't know what everything was because Marie knew almost nothing about Paris. The Eiffel Tower and the Louvre. Marie also knew that she wanted to eat snails, dripping with garlic sauce. It was Ellen's mother who had long ago urged her to try them, who had told Marie that her life would not be complete until she had. This was Marie's life. She had made it to Paris, and the snails were suddenly possible. Marie had never thought she would make it this far. She had not thought about what would happen after prison. Who she would spend her days with. Caitlin loved her goldfish.

"I want to name him Paris," she said.

"Like Paris Hilton," Marie said.

Caitlin looked confused.

"No," she said.

"Not like Paris Hilton," Marie said.

Caitlin said nothing, her expression troubled.

"Like the name of the city we are in right now?" Marie said. Caitlin nodded. To Marie's satisfaction, Benoît already seemed put out, carrying his daughter's goldfish bowl. She watched with amusement as he used one hand to get a pack of cigarettes from his jeans pocket, then to extract a cigarette and try to light it. He did not ask Marie to hold the glass bowl and she didn't offer.

Following Benoît's lead, they crossed the street bordering the Seine, and then made it down a flight of stone steps to the river, Caitlin holding Marie's hand, going slowly, one leg and then another on each wide step, step after step. She refused to be picked up, and Benoît walked quickly ahead of them, with purpose. Marie watched him walk away and wondered what would happen if they weren't able to catch up. But he stopped not far from the bottom of the stone staircase, positioning himself on the end of a long line, and Marie and Caitlin were able to join him there.

"What is this for?" Marie asked.

"We will travel by boat, I think," Benoît said. "It will be faster. You'll like it. Trust me."

Marie raised her eyebrow.

"You will like the boat," Benoît said. "Americans do."

Marie watched as Benoît Doniel paid for their tickets.

Her American dollars, so far, were still untouched.

They went to the top deck of the boat and sat on a wooden bench that looked out on the Seine. Benoît was right about something. Marie did like it. It was also a way to see Paris without walking, without Caitlin constantly slowing them down.

Coming up, she could see Notre Dame. Marie had studied the building in an art history class, in college, when she had been a different person, a student, earnest.

"Those are called flying buttresses," Marie told Caitlin.

Marie was impressed with herself, that she had remembered the term. She had never felt the need to use it before in everyday conversation. Marie wondered what else was stored in her brain.

"Those are gargoyles," Marie said, pointing to the monsters on the cathedral, too far away for Caitlin to see. "Those crazy monsters. Do you see them?"

"No," Caitlin said, leaning forward, standing on the tips of her toes. "Where are crazy monsters? Where, Marie?"

Marie pulled Caitlin back. It was impossible for Caitlin to

fall overboard, she was too small to make it over the railing, but Marie pulled Caitlin against her legs anyway and tickled her ribs. Caitlin laughed happily, forgetting about the monsters.

"No!" she screamed, delighted, as Marie tickled her.

Benoît stood next to them, leaving the goldfish bowl on the bench. He tried to light a cigarette and failed with the wind.

"That was awful. What you did. In front of me." Marie looked again at the cathedral, but somehow, what she saw instead was the pink nipple of Lili Gaudet's perfectly formed breast, the top half of her black lingerie hanging around her waist. Marie blinked and she could see the cathedral again. They were getting closer and closer. "I had assumed something about us, what we might mean to each other, and I guess that wasn't true."

Benoît Doniel said nothing. Not a thing.

Even Caitlin was quiet.

Marie had never had a fight with Juan José. She did not know how adults behaved in a situation like this. It had felt brave to Marie, to speak the unspeakable. She was giving Benoît Doniel an opening, a chance to defend himself. Earlier that same day, she had left him, turning street corners at random, moving blindly forward, but now they were on a boat together. It almost might have been romantic.

He could say something, Marie thought. Something. Anything. He had left Ellen, had left his wife, for her. Taken off with Ellen's beautiful child and her credit card. Wasn't that a sign of love? Of something? Marie turned from the view to look at him. The sight of him took her by surprise, the same wonderful face that she anticipated every morning after

Ellen left for work. The author of *Virginie at Sea* with his swoopy hair and beaky nose. Marie felt herself swell with love looking at him. Even after the French actress. She loved him. A little bit. Though she also understood that Benoît Doniel was rotten. And it was not just for sleeping with the French actress, but also because he had slept with her, Marie, the babysitter.

The boat was now directly in front of Notre Dame and it seemed to Marie that this was an incredible waste of extraordinary scenery, to be having the conversation she had started.

"I didn't plan that," Benoît said. "I would take it back. How that happened. I did not mean to ever see Lili again. It was a surprise on the airplane. I wasn't prepared. She wouldn't let me go. You saw that, Marie. I don't plan these things in my life. I never planned on you."

Marie blinked. This was his explanation? This was his big apology? This was how he conducted his life? By accident? Had Juan José planned his bank robbery? Or had he and his partner just shown up, guns waving? Marie had no idea. Why hadn't she asked him? Ellen certainly planned things. She had an elaborate plan for her life that included law school and careful control of Caitlin's diet. Had Ellen planned on Benoît Doniel? It had been a mistake, obviously, Ellen's chance encounter with her future husband in Paris. She belonged with someone altogether different, a man who dressed conservatively and kept a meticulous account ledger. Marie had never planned on running away to Paris with Ellen's husband and her daughter. She wished they could go back in time, go back three days, and stay there, forever suspended in time.

"How?" Marie wanted to know. "How did you ever write a novel?"

"What?"

"If you don't plan things?" Marie said. "How did you write *Virginie at Sea*? How did you write it?"

Benoît shook his head. He did not answer Marie's question. Marie suddenly remembered Caitlin, realized that she was no longer pressed against her legs. Where was she? Marie would blame Benoît Doniel if something happened to her. It would be his fault that he had distracted Marie from what was important, from Caitlin, who had not disappointed Marie, who remained nothing less than wonderful, but Caitlin was sitting on the bench behind them, more interested in her new goldfish than the view.

"Hi Paris," she said, talking to the fish in the glass bowl. Benoît still said nothing.

"You can't write a book by accident," Marie said.

"You're right."

"I'm right, what? You can't write a book by accident? Then how did you write it?"

"I didn't."

Marie looked at Benoît, speechless, suddenly understanding the unmistakable truth of what he had just said. He hadn't written *Virginie at Sea*. He had been lying to her, all this time. Marie bit her lip. She shook her head. She watched as Benoît tried, again, to light a cigarette. He was helpless, pathetic, the wind blowing out the flickering flame from his lighter. Marie was disgusted. She could not bear to watch him fail at this simple task, fail and keep on failing, and so she cupped her hands in front of his once beloved face, blocking the wind.

It all made perfect sense.

"Your sister wrote it," Marie said.

"Yes. *Oui. Ma sœur.*"

"Nathalie wrote *Virginie at Sea*."

The book that had spelled out Marie's innermost thoughts, that had spoken to her soul. It had been written, of course, by a woman, a sad, lost, young woman, unsure if she wanted to live or die.

"I found it," Benoît said, "after she killed herself. I found her book in a hatbox. She left me a note, telling me what to do. She left a list of publishers, their addresses, everything."

Marie looked at Benoît, at his familiar face, the one she had first learned by heart on that worn book jacket, lying on the top bunk of her prison cell, fantasizing about an imaginary author instead of a dead lover.

"What are you thinking?" Benoît said.

"She wanted you to publish the book in her name?"

"She was dead." Benoît Doniel was self-righteous in his defense. "She left me. Just checked out. Bye-bye. You understand this? How this feels? She left me with her body. I had to take care of her dead body. My *petite sœur*. I had to cut her down from the ceiling. She did not deserve to be celebrated. The book was a gift. Her gift to me. Because I had to keep living without her. It was only fair. Don't you see?"

Fair. Maybe it was. In Benoît Doniel's French fucked-up view of the world. But not even drinking coffee from a bowl, none of his ridiculous fop-headed charm, could minimize the hurt Marie felt.

"Who else knows?"

Benoît sucked on his cigarette, smoked down to the butt.

"Who?" she repeated.

"You," he said. "You and me. No one else. You and me. You and me."

The wind blew Benoît's swoopy, idiotic hair into his eyes.

He threw his cigarette butt into the Seine, polluting his own city. You and me, a pathetic attempt to save himself. If nothing else, Marie held Benoît Doniel's future in her hands. She could ruin him. Or she could walk away. Take the high road. Except that she was trapped on a slow boat going down the Seine, surrounded by water and old-world architecture.

"Do they sell drinks on this boat?" Marie asked.

"Drinks?"

"Cold beverages. Do they?"

"I don't know. They must."

"Buy me something," Marie said.

"What?"

"I don't care. A water. An Orangina. Buy me something French that I've never had before. Buy me that. Get something for Caitlin, too."

"What?"

"What? I don't know. Anything. Get her a juice," Marie said. "No, milk, get her some milk."

"Milk," Caitlin said. Marie had not known that Caitlin, safe on her bench, was listening. "I want milk."

"Milk," Marie said, though she knew Caitlin had already had too much milk. But Marie was not Caitlin's mother. Not her mother. Though not her babysitter, either, anymore. "Get her something to eat, too. She must be hungry."

Marie looked at Benoît and he looked back at her. She tilted back her head, made a drinking motion, and he left. Marie turned to watch him go and noticed, with satisfaction, a long line. She turned to look again at the view, to take in the flying buttresses and the gargoyles, to appreciate them, but Notre Dame was long gone. Marie could see the Eiffel Tower coming up instead. It seemed to be everywhere, taunting her.

The grandmother's apartment was dark and dirty and smelled horrible, like a dead animal. It was on the sixth floor of an old apartment building.

After getting off the boat, they had left the splendor of the day and gone underground, riding the metro, taking two different trains to what Benoît Doniel said was the outskirts of the city, before waiting for a bus that took them someplace even farther. The look of the people in the streets had changed. There were fewer stylish white people, wearing scarves, walking poodles. Instead, Marie heard people speaking Arabic. Instead, the streets were filled with mostly blacks, blacks and old people. Benoît told Marie the name of the neighborhood, but it was in French, complicated, and she promptly forgot it. It was not where Lili Gaudet lived.

They had climbed six flights of stairs, steep, winding, narrow, uncarpeted stairs. Benoît continued to carry the goldfish bowl; Marie had Caitlin. She had carried her all the way from the bus where she had fallen asleep. They had missed her nap time. The stroller remained in the French actress's apartment, as did the four suitcases.

"My *grandmaman*," Benoît said as he opened the door, "went into a home. Not too long ago, I think. I don't remember exactly. There is supposed to be a cleaning lady. It doesn't seem like she has been here for a while, though, does it?"

Marie could see particles of dust floating in the air.

A spindly black cat with scabs on its back came rushing at them. Mucus was dripping out of both of the cat's eyes. It went straight for Benoît, pressed itself against his legs and started to meow, the loudest meow Marie had ever heard a cat make. Marie had to suppress the urge to kick it. Benoît almost dropped the goldfish.

"Do you know this cat?" Marie said.

"Ludivine, of course. My grandmother's cat. I had forgotten all about her."

"Is that a girl's name?"

"Yes, of course."

"She's starving."

"It looks like it."

Benoît put the goldfish on top of a table and bent down to pet the miserable cat. It continued to meow, opening its mouth wide. Ludivine was missing her front teeth. If she didn't shut up, she would wake Caitlin. Caitlin needed to sleep. Marie had been grateful when she had conked out on the bus.

"This is where we are going to stay?"

They stood in the hallway, unwilling to go farther, the cat screeching. Marie had been looking forward to laying Caitlin down, but she changed her mind, afraid that the cat might try to eat the girl.

Already, Marie missed the French actress's apartment. It was clean and light and had sleek, modern furniture. A clean bathtub. A balcony in the room where she had had sex with Benoît. The room where Benoît had proceeded to have sex with the French actress.

"Are you sure she is in a home?"

Marie almost expected to find an old woman, eyes chewed out, body decomposing. She reluctantly followed Benoît down the hall. They passed through a living room, which was dark, the blinds drawn, and stepped into the kitchen. The bad smell grew fouler with every step. There were rotten onions on the floor of the kitchen, cardboard boxes and newspapers and bags ripped to shreds. Jars of spices, boxes of pasta, all of them on the floor. Chewed upon cans of cat food. Marie could see the bite marks on the metal.

This, of course, was also Paris.

Ludivine had followed them into the kitchen, rubbing against their legs, plaintively meowing. Marie stepped on her tail and nearly dropped Caitlin.

The cat started to chew on one of the closed cans. She obviously had no faith in Benoît Doniel, either. In the midst of the mess, Marie saw the long, sharp teeth on the floor, the two front teeth missing from Ludivine's mouth. There was also an empty water bowl.

Marie gently lay Caitlin down on top of a wooden kitchen table, hoping not to wake her up. Caitlin opened her eyes. "Hi Marie," she said.

"Stay there," Marie said.

"The cat is meowing, Marie," Caitlin said.

"I know it is. I'm going to feed the cat and maybe it will be quiet."

"It's hungry? That cat?" Caitlin sat up. She rubbed her eyes.

Marie nodded.

"Do you know where a can opener is?" she asked Benoît.

Benoît only shrugged. He pulled a chair from the table and sat down, lit another cigarette, filling the already airless, bad-smelling room with smoke.

"*Mon Dieu*," he said. He was less than useless.

"Will you help me look for it?" Marie heard how she sounded. The nagging tone of an aggrieved wife.

"Help me," she repeated. It was not a question.

Benoît got up. He began to open drawers, rifling through random objects. "I don't see it," he said. "There is none."

Marie was silent. He had brought them here, to this place. He had said the words "grandmother's apartment" and Marie had pictured crocheted rugs, a freshly baked quiche lorraine, bowls of hot chocolate.

Benoît kept looking, eventually finding the can opener in a crowded drawer. He handed it to Marie.

"I need a plate," she said, and Benoît found that, too. Marie opened the cat food, pushing Ludivine away with one hand, afraid that the cat would bite her, which, of course, the cat couldn't do because she had no teeth. But Marie didn't want to touch or be touched by that miserable creature. She practically threw the plate on the floor and watched, dispassionately, as Ludivine pounced.

"The cat is eating!" Caitlin thought this was exciting.

"She was hungry," Marie said.

Marie was also hungry.

Benoît stared at Ludivine as she ate the food. In seconds, it was gone. Marie opened another can. She knelt down and pushed Ludivine away with her elbow. She put more food on the plate.

"Here, cat," she said.

Ludivine did not seem like a good name for a cat.

The cat stepped away from the fresh plate of food and proceeded to vomit.

"Marie, Marie!"

"What is it, Caty Bean?"

"Is the cat sick?"

"She is," Marie said. "Maybe she ate too fast. I don't know. She's not healthy, that's for sure." Marie looked at

Benoît. He didn't move. He smoked his cigarette, like the ridiculous French person that he was. He wasn't going to clean
up the vomit. But it wasn't Marie's cat. She wasn't going to
do it. Marie looked out of the kitchen, down the hallway: an
apartment full of potential horrors.

"What else are we going to find here?" Marie asked.

A dead body behind one of the closed doors still seemed
entirely possible. There was a knock at the front door.

"Aha," Marie said.

Benoît looked at Marie. The knocking continued.

"Benoît," a female voice called out. "*C'est toi?* Benoît?"

The knocking continued.

Marie wasn't going to let this woman in. Not another
woman from Benoît's past. Instead, she opened the refrigerator. Earlier that morning, before leaving the French actress's
apartment, she had opened her refrigerator. She'd found two
eggs, three bottles of chilled champagne, Dijon mustard, and
a box of raspberries. Vanilla ice cream in the freezer. Marie
also had a mental image of Ellen's stainless-steel refrigerator,
always crammed full of good food.

The grandmother's refrigerator was empty. Clean. Cleaned
out. A box of baking soda and nothing else. Marie breathed
in the chemical smell of cleanser and started to cough. She
slammed the refrigerator door shut. There was no air in
the room, only Benoît Doniel's rancid cigarette smoke. The
kitchen windows were closed. Marie tried to open a window,
but it was locked. The locks in France were different.

"I want off," Caitlin said.

She stood up on the table.

Marie went to Caitlin and scooped her off the table;
Caitlin locked her legs around Marie's waist. She was getting

heavier. Soon, she would need dinner. She would need a bath. Marie would need dinner. Marie would need a bath. The cat, done vomiting, returned to the plate of food as if she had never gotten sick. The knocking continued.

"Are you going to open the door?" Marie asked Benoît.

"I don't know. Should I?"

"Benoît?" the woman called.

Another goddamned Frenchwoman. If Marie met another one like the French actress, she would start to miss Ellen.

"You better open it," Marie said. "She knows we are in here."

This one had dark curly hair. She was older and wore a shapeless green cardigan and a black shapeless skirt, a beaded necklace. She was overweight, had a mole on her cheek, a sharp black hair growing from its center.

Marie watched the inevitable cheek kissing, and then a long, sad hug. She did not know how long Benoît Doniel had been away or why he had left. He had left his country behind. He must have meant it, to leave everyone and everything behind: the old grandmother, the demented French actress, the memory of his dead sister, the book he had stolen.

The hug with this frumpy, distressed Frenchwoman finally ended and then she began to speak to Benoît. In urgent French, of course. Everyone was always speaking French. Marie found it maddening. She could read nothing in Benoît's face, whose blank expression did not change though the woman grew more and more passionate. Big news, obviously, was being shared.

"Who is that?" Caitlin said. Marie shook her head, but Caitlin seemed to lose interest in the question the moment she asked it. "My shirt is dirty."

Caitlin held out her arm. There was something red on the sleeve of her shirt. Marie recognized the breakfast jam.

"That's okay," Marie said. "We'll clean it."

Marie hoped that the woman would leave soon, or at least offer them something to eat. Marie noticed a break in the conversation. Benoît was sweating through his untucked shirt.

"Come," he said to Marie. "This is Sophie. Marie."

The woman appeared embarrassed; she had not noticed Marie or Caitlin. And because she was French, she went straight for Marie's cheeks. They were both kissed. There was nothing Marie could do. The woman then tousled Caitlin's hair.

"No," Caitlin said.

"*Parlez-vous Français?*" she asked Marie.

Marie shook her head.

"*Domage.*"

"Sophie lives next door," Benoît said. "The nursing home had her telephone number. My grandmother died two days ago."

"Fuck," Marie said.

"Fuck," Caitlin said.

"She died?" Marie said.

"She died," Benoît said.

"But not here?"

Marie did not want Caitlin to see a dead body.

"At the nursing home. They need me to tell them what to do with the body. They have been waiting."

Sophie in the cardigan sweater started talking in French again, waving her arms, growing louder and louder, before enfolding Benoît in her arms, because he suddenly began to weep.

"Daddy is crying?" Caitlin said.

"He's a writer," Marie answered. "He's very sensitive. It's okay, Kit Kat. It's okay."

Ludivine had come back to where they all stood and started to meow. This roused Benoît. He knelt down and began to pet the wretched cat.

"*Pauvre chat*," he said, shaking his head.

Benoît Doniel would not know what to do. Marie understood this. He would need a woman to tell him what came next. But Marie did not feel that this was her job. He had taken her to Paris; it was his town. He was supposed to be responsible for their well-being, Marie and Caitlin. The Frenchwoman continued to talk at Benoît, unaware that he was beyond helpless; she thrust at him various pieces of paper.

"I am going to have to pay for the cremation," Benoît told Marie, still petting the cat. "And take care of this apartment. I have to pay her bills and get rid of her things. I am the only one left. Another body, Marie, I am supposed to take care of. I am not strong enough for this."

The telephone in the grandmother's apartment started to ring. It rang and it rang.

"I am the only one left," Benoît repeated.

Marie felt no sympathy. Who was she? And Caitlin? He wasn't alone. Unless he knew how much she could not bear to look at him, her fury so enormous. Marie hoped that would change. It was Sophie who put her hand on Benoît's arm. She said something of consolation to him, in French, of course. Which was fine with Marie. She had not signed up for this. She had not signed up for being lied to, cheated on, and certainly not this, an all-out emotional collapse.

The telephone continued to ring.

"*Réponds au téléphone?*" the frumpy Frenchwoman said.

Marie could hear the anxiety in her voice. The ringing phone made Marie want to jump out of her skin. She could hear the desperation on the other end, the insistence of the ringing.

"Don't answer it," Marie said, surprised by her instinct, still, to protect him. Protect herself.

Benoît went down the hall of the apartment, disappearing into another room.

"*Oui?*" Marie heard Benoît say.

And then silence. A long, heavy silence, broken only by Ludivine's plaintive meows, until Marie heard Benoît Doniel put the phone back onto the receiver. He returned, slowly, dejected, down the hall.

"Ellen," he said to Marie. "That was Ellen."

Sophie responded again in rapid French.

Benoît put his hand up, as if to push her away.

Marie felt her heart start to race. She stepped away from the front door, almost expecting Ellen to come bursting through. What did she say, Ellen? Where was she? Paris? New York? What did she say? What did she plan to do?

"What did she say?" Marie asked.

She wanted to smack Benoît Doniel, for making her ask. She would have smacked him, but felt hesitant in front of the Frenchwoman, a witness to their disintegration.

"What did she say?"

Benoît's face had turned a shade of ashy green. His swoopy hair was stuck to his forehead, which was covered with a slick sheen of nervous sweat. He did not answer Marie. He picked up Caitlin and started heading toward the door.

"Down," Caitlin said.

Benoît did not put her down.

"Get the cat," he told Marie.

"No," Marie said.

Benoît picked up the cat.

"I want my goldfish," Caitlin said. "I want Paris."

"The fucking goldfish," Benoît said. "Fine."

He rushed past Marie and the Frenchwoman, still holding Caitlin and the cat. He managed to also grab the goldfish bowl from the kitchen, and then he made for the door. "Come," he said to Marie.

"What did she say?" Marie demanded.

Benoît Doniel was already taking the steps, two at a time.

"We have to go," Marie explained to the dumpy French-woman whose mouth was wide open, who had finally stopped talking. At least, she could still say "we."

Marie stepped out of the dead grandmother's apartment. She watched Benoît make his escape. Halfway down the first flight of steps, Benoît dropped the cat, but he kept his grip on Caitlin and the goldfish. Ludivine ran ahead and then waited. Marie followed, slowly, hands empty, down the six flights of stairs, one step at a time.

Ludivine ran rapid circles around the back of the taxi, meowing loudly. The cabdriver cursed at Benoît and Benoît cursed back. The exchange was in French, again, so Marie could tune them out, and Caitlin could not mimic back the words. Not yet. Benoît could not catch the demented cat. He grabbed hold of her at one point, and Ludivine dragged a claw across his cheek, leaving behind a long thin line of blood.

"Fuck," Benoît said, reverting to English.

"Daddy cursed," Caitlin said.

"Why did you bring her?" Marie said. "We can't even take care of ourselves."

It was like all of that luggage that had traveled across the Atlantic Ocean. Benoît had no idea what should be left behind; he didn't know how to start a new life. He'd already gone back to a past mistake, the French actress, Lili Gaudet. Ludivine was an ugly, scary cat.

Luckily, Caitlin seemed to think that it was all a game, all of it. She still expected her mother to tuck her in at the end of a long day at the office. She had not properly grasped how her life had changed. She sat in Marie's lap. No car seat, which remained in the brownstone in New York. The taxi didn't even have seat belts, but this time, Caitlin didn't ask.

"Kitty, kitty, kitty," she said, laughing. "The kitty is running."

Marie looked at Benoît Doniel, furious. Not about the French actress or the novel that he had stolen from his dead sister, but their current predicament. That very moment in time. Marie was furious about the dead grandmother, furious that he'd dragged them on public transportation to that horrid apartment, for not providing them dinner the moment Marie realized she was hungry. For the fact that they had already been discovered. Ellen had already tracked him to his grandmother's apartment in Paris. There was no telling what else she might know.

Ellen seemed to know things about her husband that Marie did not. There was a time when Marie and Ellen used to share important information, when they used to study for tests and bake chocolate chip cookies together.

"I can take care of us," Benoît said, but he was breathing fast, too fast, like he might have a heart attack. His eyes were panicked, darting around the taxi, following Ludivine's mad dash. He put a hand to his cheek and he wiped off the blood. Marie reached for his hand and held it tight.

"*Merci*," he said.

Marie did not let go.

The trip back into the city was much quicker than the ride out. The cat was finally calming down, pacing back and forth by the back window. Marie almost recognized the streets they passed through. When the taxi stopped, they were back at Lili Gaudet's apartment.

"No," Marie said.

"We go to a hotel," Benoît said, "and Ellen calls the credit card people, and she finds us. *Voilà. Fini.* All over. Our *grande* love affair. *Un désastre. Merde, merde, merde. C'est tout.*"

Even Benoît Doniel was speaking French now. For no reason. He was talking to her, Marie.

"She found you at your grandmother's house," Marie pointed out. "Why not at Lili's?"

"She does not know about Lili."

That was something. But not enough. Benoît, he was not smart enough to outmaneuver his wife. Plus, he had no money of his own.

"What is *merde*?" Caitlin asked.

Marie smiled. The kid was picking up French curses already. She was a smart one. A wonder. "I've got money. Cash, dollars," Marie said to Benoît. "I'll pay for the hotel. I'll pay. We can go to a hotel. We can take a bath."

Benoît looked at Marie, at last, with genuine interest.

"Maybe," he said. "*Peut-être.* A hotel. You have money? How much do you have?" He didn't wait for Marie's answer, putting his hands into his pocket, coming back out with a wad of crumpled euros. "First, I must have a drink."

He paid for the taxi, and they stepped outside onto the cobblestone street, Benoît holding the ridiculous, awful, exhausted cat, Marie taking Caitlin's hand. They had returned, at least, to the real Paris; they'd made it out of that awful netherworld. The cab sped from the curb, so fast Marie was startled. She had Caitlin, they were still holding hands, tight. She still had her backpack. Marie was not sure when they had lost Caitlin's travel bag. At the café. On the boat. The subway.

"Paris!" Caitlin cried. Neither Benoît or Marie understood. "Paris." Tears welled in her eyes. It was a miracle, Marie thought, that she hadn't started crying before this.

"What is it?" Maris said. "What is it, Caty Bean? We are in Paris. Are you hungry? You are tired?"

"My fish. Paris."

They had lost the goldfish, too. Benoît had carried it down the six flights of steps, but he must have left it on the curb, getting them into the taxi.

"That goldfish," Benoît said to Marie, as Caitlin began to cry in earnest, "was my worst idea yet."

"I can think of worse ones," Marie said.

"Don't be cruel."

"No," Marie said, her voice sarcastic, noticing for the first time the long bloody scratch on her arm, also courtesy of Ludivine. "I would never be mean. Not to you."

Benoît bent down on his knees, looking Caitlin in the eyes. "It's okay, *ma petite*. Now we have a cat. This is even better. You can pet Ludivine. Okay? You want to have a cat of your own?"

He held out Ludivine for Caitlin to see. The cat was also missing clumps of hair. One eye had crusted shut. Marie didn't want Caitlin to touch it. She shook her head at Caitlin and Caitlin didn't.

"You don't like the cat?" Benoît said.

Caitlin shook her head.

"Okay," Benoît said. "Don't touch her. Let's get drinks. Drinks. Do you want milk?" he asked Caitlin.

"Yes."

Caitlin always wanted milk.

"We'll get you some macaroni and cheese," Marie said, aware that this was a promise she might not be able to keep. They headed into the restaurant, the same from the night before. Benoît ordered a beer before sitting down, taking the menus from the waiter's hand. He did not ask what Marie wanted.

"For me, too," Marie said. "Beer. And milk." She pointed to Caitlin. "Please."

The waiter gave Marie a nasty look. In a crisis, was Marie supposed to suddenly pretend to know the language? Throw in a *merci*? She would not. He could understand her perfectly well. He said something to Benoît about *le chat* and a heated conversation ensued, the waiter pointing at the door. His voice was raised. Marie could see what looked like a manager heading toward them.

"I need your bag," Benoît said to Marie.

"Why?"

Marie's backpack was stuffed full with her worldly belongings. She owned nothing but for the contents of that bag. But Benoît grabbed it, unzipped the main compartment, and began emptying it, piling all of Marie's private, personal things onto their table. The restaurant was simple but elegant, a gleaming bar, mirrors, wood tables, a plate-glass window that looked onto the street.

"Don't," Marie said.

She watched as the pile continued to grow. Her favorite pair of jeans, her plain white cotton underwear, balls of matched striped socks, Ellen's crumpled silk kimono, her copy of *Virginie at Sea*. Marie's beloved little book from prison, it was still a real thing, a physical object, despite the disturbing truth Marie had recently learned. Marie watched the novel disappear into the pile, beneath a red dress, a couple of T-shirts, a stack of letters held together with a rubber band. The letters were from Juan José, the ones she had received in prison, only three, everything that he had ever written to Marie before his suicide, none of them ever hinting that he might take his own life.

More underwear emerged from the bag, a bottle of coconut shampoo. Her toothbrush and toothpaste in a plastic Ziploc bag. Three silver bangles. Marie's entire existence was spread out on the table at the French restaurant for the world to see, a small, sad accumulation of objects that represented her life.

Marie was ashamed, embarrassed to see her life spread out for view like pieces of sordid junk. Thirty years.

Benoît Doniel grabbed Ludivine by the neck and stuffed her inside the empty backpack. Marie had not forgotten the image of the cat vomiting up a fresh can of cat food, mucus dripping from her eyes. Benoît zipped the bag shut. The cat meowed mournfully, but she didn't struggle. Maybe she would go ahead and die. Maybe all the struggle was gone from her after the taxi ride. Beautiful French people in the restaurant were looking at them, the din of conversation had died out, but the waiter, at least, accepted Benoît's solution, cat in the bag. He left their table and when he returned, he was bearing beer. And milk for Caitlin.

Benoît ordered another beer as the waiter set the fresh drinks on the table, carefully placing them on the edge, away from Marie's unfortunate pile.

"*Merci beaucoup,*" Benoît said.

Marie had loved to listen to Juan José in Mexico, speaking

Spanish. She had marveled at another side of the man she did not yet know. But every new revelation about Benoît Doniel was more unwelcome than the last.

The three of them sat quietly drinking. There really was nothing to say. The beer was cold, good, better than any other beer she had ever drunk before. Even in Mexico. Maybe it was the glass, which looked like something Marie would expect to drink champagne from. The beer was so good Marie regretted the wine she drank the night before. Caitlin was also happy with her milk, which supposedly was also better. Europe was supposedly a superior continent in so many ways; it was unfortunate that Marie's current situation felt so hopeless.

Marie's belongings were still on the table. The beer had not changed that. She wanted to put them away, but did not see how that was possible. She'd have to get rid of the cat. She wanted to get rid of the cat.

"Who are you?" Benoît said.

Marie had forgotten, in a way, that Benoît Doniel was still there. That they were talking to each other. She had begun to think about Mexico, how simple it was there. No money had been required to live in that small oceanside village, though Juan José had had a suitcase full of just that.

Marie looked at him, irritated.

"What did you say?"

"I'm sorry," he said. "I have no idea who you are. Half of the things you own, you have stolen from my wife. You have my daughter on your lap. She seems to like you. And my life is ruined. And I am not sure how this happened. Because you fell in love with my sister's book."

Marie nodded.

His life was ruined.

He did not know who *she* was.

Marie's beer was empty so she reached for his. Marie didn't know how to fight back. She had never fought with Juan José. She had fought with Ellen, as a child, but these were brief, violent spats. Pushing and shoving, and one time, which Marie was never allowed to forget, biting. She had drawn blood from Ellen's skinny arm, she could not remember why. Marie had won the fight, but it hadn't felt like a victory. Ellen had run all the way home and Marie had been forced by her mother to apologize. Later, Ellen's mother had given Marie a lecture about anger management. No one, for a second, thought that Marie might have had a reason to bite her friend.

Marie could not fight Benoît Doniel in this lovely restaurant. She could bite his arm, she could draw blood, as if she were still nine years old, but she could not win. She had already lost. Marie didn't love Benoît anymore, at least not the way she had only the day before. Not the way she had loved the idea of him, when he was only a black-and-white photo on a book jacket.

He did not understand how sad this made her, the change between them.

Benoît reached for the silver bangles on the table; he slid them over his own wrist. "These bracelets," he said. "They were Nathalie's. Did you know?" Marie shook her head. She had not known. She wanted Nathalie's bracelets. She wanted them back. "I gave them to my wife. My wife."

Marie drank more of Benoît's beer.

"We'll need another," she said. "You'll need to order another one for me, too."

Marie looked at the bracelets on Benoît's wrist with longing, knowing that she would never get them back. They had been Nathalie's. He should never have given them to Ellen; they were meant to be Marie's.

Ludivine meowed, sorrowfully, from the floor, from inside Marie's knapsack, and Marie felt the bile rise in the back of her throat. She was able somehow to force the rising vomit to go back down. The taste in her mouth was putrid. She drank more of Benoît's beer. She drank and drank until the tall glass was empty.

"We need something to eat," she whispered. "And water."

In her other life, Juan José had brought Marie home to meet his mother. A chicken had been killed on her behalf and turned into a marvelous stew. The family had taken Marie to their church. They had accepted her as one of their own, a beloved child. They expected nothing from her, except to be pretty, to make Juan José happy. Marie closed her eyes. What would Ruby Hart do? If they were in the laundry, folding and washing and talking, what would she say about this short, skinny Frenchman, blaming her for all of his problems? Ruby would tell Marie how it was. *You and this man*, she'd say, *you are done, you are so done, girl.*

She'd also tell Marie to give up the little girl. Give up Caitlin and the dream of a happy life, stolen from another woman. *Make your own life.* That is what she would say. By the time Ruby was released from prison, she would have her law degree. Marie looked at Caitlin, drinking her milk. She did not want to give her up. Ruby Hart had killed her husband. He had probably deserved it, but she was in no position to give advice.

Marie saw the waiter approaching the table. She put her hand on Benoît's arm. "Can you order something for us, please?"

Marie didn't want to ask Benoît for anything, ever again, but also she couldn't imagine talking to that dreadful man, the waiter. He had all the power in the world: to bring her food or deny it.

"Don't tell me what to do," Benoît said.

But Benoît hailed the waiter. He ordered two more beers and, not even looking at the menu, ordered food for all of them. Marie smiled at him, grateful, and almost immediately wished that she hadn't. Benoît reached for the kimono on the table, pressing the silk fabric to his cheek.

"You really are a thief," he said.

It had made sense for Marie to take the kimono. Of all the belongings that had come out of her backpack, this had been Marie's favorite. She thought of it as her own. She had worn it after their baths, before she and Benoît made love. Benoît would pull on the sash, open the flaps of silk, and watch, almost reverent, as it fell to the floor.

"My grandmother needs to be cremated," Benoît said. "Her apartment needs to be cleaned. Her bill at the nursing home needs to be settled. My wife knows that I am here. That I ran off with the babysitter. She is coming to France. She is coming. I walked out on Lili. Again. After making love to her. For the second time in my life, I have walked out on her. I don't know if she will forgive me this time."

Marie looked at Benoît Doniel, plagiarist, blankly.

He was worried about Ellen, his wife.

He was worried about Lili. He was worried about Lili, his former lover. His present lover, too. He had just admitted to that.

Marie did not exist.

You and me, he had said on the boat.

Ludivine meowed again from inside Marie's backpack. They could be arrested for animal abuse. The meows had become weaker, less frequent. The cat very well might die in this Paris restaurant. Marie would have to carry this dead cat with her for the rest of her life.

Marie drank more beer.

It was something to do.

The beer was already starting to get warm. She needed to drink more quickly.

"What did Ellen say?" Marie said. "In New York? What did she say about me?"

"Who are you?" Benoît looked at Marie as if he might spit in her face. "A criminal. You just got out of prison. What was I thinking?" He shook his head with disgust. "You are very pretty, you know. You have big tits."

Marie felt tears spring to her eyes, as if she had been hit. She turned away from Benoît and smiled at Caitlin, who never liked to see anyone cry.

"Hey there Kit Kat."

The nickname seemed wrong with Ludivine suffocating beneath the table.

"Are you crying?" Caitlin asked.

Marie shook her head.

"Me?" she said. "No way. Not me. I don't cry. Never ever. I am a tough, hardened criminal."

Caitlin stood up on her chair. She leaned over and wiped a tear from Marie's face.

"Your food is coming," Marie told Caitlin. "Something good to eat. Something French and delicious. What did you order for her?" she asked Benoît. "Something she'll like?"

Benoît Doniel shrugged.

"Something delicious," Marie said to Caitlin. "You'll see. Better than macaroni and cheese."

Caitlin wiped another tear from Marie's face.

"Where is Mommy?"

Marie wiped an imaginary tear off of Caitlin's cheek.

"She's on her way now," Marie said. "What did you think? She just left the office. She's on her way. She works too hard, your mother."

The waiter arrived with the food.

He looked at the table, covered with Marie's things. Marie looked at Benoît. "You figure it out," she said. "You have already humiliated me."

Benoît pushed her things onto the extra chair at the table, much of the haphazard pile falling to the floor. The displeased waiter continued to look displeased, but he served them their food. Benoît had ordered some kind of pasta, small shells covered in a cream sauce. It was a French macaroni and cheese: mild, smooth, easy to slide down. The waiter had brought the same dish for Caitlin, only in a smaller bowl.

Marie and Benoît and Caitlin, they ate in silence. Marie was grateful for the food, grateful that she did not need to decide what to eat, that Benoît did know, without having to ask, what she would like. They had sat like this in Ellen's kitchen, eating companionably; there had been no animosity, only an unhurried calm, pleasure. As Benoît began to eat his pasta, she could feel a change in him, the hatred easing from his body.

He had never spoken that way before, about her tits.

"Forgive me," he said. He actually ruffled Marie's hair. "Please. I brought you here, didn't I? Forgive me. I don't know who I am anymore. Do you know?"

Marie didn't.

Benoît looked at the bangles on his wrist, touched them with affection. "Ellen never wore these, did she?"

Marie shook her head.

"She did not like them, though she would never say so."

"They are beautiful."

"My grandmother used to make this dish."

There were small peas in the sauce. Bits of bacon.

The next time the waiter came around, Benoît ordered a cognac and coffee.

"I want moose," Caitlin said, and he ordered that, too.

"I like this restaurant." Benoît Doniel leaned back in his chair, lighting a cigarette.

Outside the window, Marie observed Lili Gaudet walk past. She was wearing heels, a long skirt, a silver coat, red lipstick. Her long blond hair was loose and blew in the wind. She looked glamorous, like a movie star. She was accompanied by an older man, equally well dressed, who held her by the elbow, and just like that, they were gone. Benoît followed Marie's gaze, in time to see Lili Gaudet disappear into the night.

"She looks devastated," Benoît noted, his voice flat. Disappointed, perhaps. Marie could not tell.

The waiter put the check on the table.

Benoît picked it up and put it back down.

"I charge it?" he asked.

"You have no money? Nothing?"

"*Rien,*" he said. He held out empty hands. "I spent everything I had on the taxi."

"I have money," Marie offered. "I'll pay. And then, we can go to a hotel. Okay? Please?"

Benoît nodded, drinking his cognac.

The waiter accepted her American dollars. Given the poor exchange rate and the beer and the coffee and Caitlin's milk, the cognac and the dessert, it was more expensive than Marie had known was possible for one simple meal.

The hotel cost more than two hundred euros for the night.
Marie felt something close to panic as she handed over the money, fresh, colorful euros recently changed at an all-night market. She was even less happy to hand over her passport, but the clerk would not give them the room without it. She felt like a homeless person in the bright hotel lobby, carrying her belongings in paper shopping bags.

There was no bathtub in the room.

"There is no bathtub," Marie said.

The disappointment floored her.

"It's no problem," Benoît said, and the worst part was that to him it was not a problem.

Marie would have to bathe Caitlin either in the sink or the shower. She was prepared at least; she had bought a package of diapers at the market. They had cost twenty euros. She had spent close to fifty euros stocking up on things she thought she might need: a bar of chocolate with hazelnuts, a small wheel of Brie, a baguette, a salami, a jar of mashed apricots, milk, vanilla yogurt. A bottle of wine.

"It's a good thing," Benoît said, "I found myself a woman with money."

Marie was certain this relationship would not last another day. The strain had been too much: death, infidelity, cat abuse, plagiarism, and now this added worry about money. Also, they were drunk, still, from dinner.

Benoît lay down on the bed, shoes on.

"Caitlin needs to get ready for bed," Marie said.

Benoît looked at her but did not move.

Marie took Caitlin into the bathroom without a tub and changed her diaper. In the early days, when she was first learning her job, Caitlin needed to remind Marie, but those days were over. Marie knew when Caitlin needed to be changed. She could smell it, and she could usually anticipate it before she could smell it.

Marie had forgotten to buy wipes. She used a hotel face towel to wipe off a smear of yellow shit from Caitlin's soft bottom. Caitlin's poo smelled like the sauce from their dinner, like white wine and Parmesan cheese.

"I want my pink nightgown," Caitlin said. "My pink one."

Caitlin's pink nightgown was in Lili Gaudet's apartment. If they were lucky. Marie had no idea if Benoît had packed it. What she realized, though, was that when they woke up the next day, she would have nothing for Caitlin: no clean clothes, no stroller, no toys to play with. Marie had lasted three months with Juan José. Now, she was grateful that they had made it through the day. The idea of tomorrow filled Marie with panic. Ellen, she knew, Ellen would be coming to Paris. She could be landing at that very moment; she could already be on her way to the French police.

"You're all clean," she said to Caitlin.

Caitlin was happy to be clean. She ran out of the bathroom naked except for a fresh diaper, and Marie was struck, again, by how perfect she was. It was almost a travesty to put Caitlin in clothes, cover up her soft, peach-colored skin. Hide those chubby legs, her bony rib cage. Her little belly button.

Benoît had turned on the television, filling the room with unwanted noise, the sounds of French people speaking to one another in French. It made no sense how angry this made Marie. Benoît was eating Marie's bar of hazelnut chocolate. She watched as her backpack inched off the bed and fell to the floor with a loud thud. The entire time Marie had been changing Caitlin's diaper, Benoît had not even liberated his grandmother's hateful cat. Marie knelt down and unzipped the bag. Ludivine came running out. She stopped in front of the chest of drawers, looked around, and then immediately started to meow.

"Why did you take this miserable cat?" Marie asked.

"She belonged to my grandmother," Benoît said.

Until that afternoon, Marie had not known that Benoît Doniel had a grandmother. He had never mentioned a cat. Marie didn't know what to do with this man, now that she had successfully maneuvered him into the hotel room. She had been trying to keep him away from the French actress, but the French actress was out on a date with another man. An older man. Probably a rich man. That was how much she cared about Benoît. Marie looked at Benoît, the floppy hair, the beaky nose, and she felt tired.

"Do you have good memories?" Marie asked. "About your grandmother? Did you love her?"

Benoît thought about this question.

"She always wore funny hats that tied beneath her head. She smelled like lavender. When I was a boy, she used to tell me that I had to toughen up. That I acted like a girl. She used to make me cry. She would bake special treats and give them to Nathalie. Not me."

"This cat is pure poison," Marie said.

She turned her backpack inside out. The cat had peed in her bag. The room was beginning to smell like cat pee. Ludivine continued to meow, opening her mouth to show the toothless gap.

"I don't know why I took her. It feels like I am leaving everything behind."

"We can throw her out the window," Marie said.

"You did not just say that."

"No," Marie said. "I didn't."

Marie and Benoît stared at each other. The scab on his cheek had hardened, six or seven small dark red splotches in a neat line. Any good feeling that had been restored between them while they'd eaten creamy pasta with peas was gone again. They stared at each other with mutual loathing. Nothing else.

"Loodie is meowing," Caitlin said.

Marie looked at Caitlin, alarmed by her proximity to the crazed cat. She poured some of the milk she had bought for Caitlin into a hotel ashtray and put it on the floor for the cat Benoît would not take care of. Ludivine went for the milk and the meowing stopped.

"That's much better," Benoît said.

"Marie," Caitlin said.

"Yes, baby."

"I want my pink nightgown."

Marie nodded.

"I know you do." She began to rifle through her paper bags for something that might work. She found a red tank top, her favorite red tank top. She had had it before prison, had worn it in Mexico. With Juan José. More and more, she was thinking about Juan José.

"Hold up your arms," she said.

Caitlin held up her arms, reminding Marie why she loved her. The tank top fit her like a long, snug dress.

"That's pretty good, isn't it?" Marie said. "You look pretty in red."

"I look pretty," Caitlin said.

"We used to visit her," Benoît said. "At the sea. My grandmother. She used to rent a house, in the summers, on the sea."

"Like in your book?" Marie stopped herself. "Your sister's book?"

"Everyone in France goes away in the summer."

He was right, Benoît Doniel, not to talk about it. Marie felt an impulse that could only be described as violent when she remembered again how he had betrayed her. She had loved the author, the one with the swoopy hair and unmarked face. She could care less about the real man, his shoes on the bed. She did not want to know about his childhood.

"Do you think she left you any money?"

Benoît shook his head. "You saw how she lived," he said. "She was poor. I did not know how bad it had gotten. I don't even know if she owns that apartment. Sophie had papers to give me. I left without taking them. I am an idiot."

"Do you have any money? Besides that? Any at all?"

Benoît shook his head.

"No savings? No bank account?"

Benoît shook his head.

"The only money I ever had was from *Virginie at Sea*. I used that up years ago."

Marie lifted Caitlin onto the bed. Caitlin crawled over to Benoît, lying down next to him. Benoît fingered the strap of the red tank top.

"This is ridiculous," he said. "I'll go get her a nightgown."

"How?"

Benoît got up, suddenly, as if there had been a reason all along that he had never taken off his shoes.

"I'll be right back," he said.

Marie looked at him with horror.

"No," she said.

"I'll get our things."

"I won't forgive you. Not for this."

"I'll come right back."

Marie shook her head. He was leaving her. She felt her mouth drop open. She would not beg. She would not beg him to stay. She had nothing but contempt for Benoît Doniel, but still, this did not seem possible. He was leaving her.

"You have my daughter," he said. "I will be right back."

"Ten minutes?" Marie said.

"Yes." Benoît looked at his watch. "Maybe a little more. Twenty. Twenty minutes."

And then he was gone. He fled the hotel room like he had fled his grandmother's apartment. Desperately seeking escape. He left without kissing Marie good-bye, without even a pause for Caitlin, who had fallen asleep on top of the covers. Ellen had not kissed her daughter, either, the day they had left for Paris.

Twenty minutes, he'd said.

Marie looked at the clock.

She pulled the covers back, and gently put Caitlin beneath them. She kissed Caitlin's forehead, and thought of all the things she had done wrong. She watched Ludivine lap up her milk from the ashtray.

"Long day," Marie said.

Benoît Doniel had left her. Already, two minutes had passed.

On the television, there was a French rock band playing to a crowded stadium. Marie reached for the remote control; she was going to turn it off, but instead, she changed the channel. The channels were all French, channel after channel, even the American films and TV shows she recognized were in French, until she came to CNN World News. News of the world. Marie could not remember the last time she had taken any interest in anything besides herself. She turned off the television.

Ludivine jumped onto the bed and started to wash herself. She licked her leg with a scratchy pink tongue.

"I'm sorry, cat," Marie told her, "but you are not my problem."

Marie picked up Ludivine, holding her as far away from her body as she could, and put her outside the door to the hotel room, locking it behind her.

The meowing started right away, plaintive, sad, as if the cat had no real expectations. She had been abandoned in an apartment, after all, left to die, been rescued, tossed into a moving taxi, and then stuffed into an airless backpack. Now this. Eventually she would have to give up.

Instead, Ludivine started to scratch on the door, the sound of her claws ripping into the wood as bad as the meows. And then, finally, the noise stopped. Marie counted to ten. She opened the door. Ludivine had fallen asleep on the doormat. Marie closed the door behind her.

She felt guilty.

Guilt was almost as bad as regret. She picked up the empty ashtray and refilled it with more of Caitlin's milk and put it on the floor in the hallway, next to the sleeping cat.

Marie went back into the room. She didn't know what came next. She sat down at the end of the bed and watched Caitlin sleep. She looked at her watch. Benoît had been gone for fifteen minutes. The French actress lived less than three blocks away. Marie calculated: eight minutes to get there, eight minutes to return to the hotel, five minutes of conversation. That was all she deserved. Which meant that Benoît would be back soon.

Marie pulled back the curtains in front of the window. The window opened to a balcony with a view of the Eiffel Tower, which lit up the sky. She had had no idea.

Marie looked back into the room. Benoît Doniel was still gone; Caitlin was asleep. Marie was all alone with the famous monument. She had expected to feel a great sense of wonder, seeing the Eiffel Tower with her own eyes, but she couldn't register the appropriate emotion. Marie had taken a boat trip down the Seine, but what had made a greater impression was Ludivine's heap of steaming vomit on the kitchen floor.

Marie leaned her arms against the balcony railing, nodding to herself. She had made it. She was not in a prison cell. She was not in her mother's sad, dirty house, staring at the walls. She was breathing fresh air, her long hair blowing in the wind, standing in front of the Eiffel Tower. It *was* beautiful. She could see that, even if it did not make her feel happy. She still recognized it. The beauty.

Marie could go there, the Eiffel Tower. She could go tomorrow. Marie did not need to be afraid. She could look forward to the coming day.

Marie would wake up in Paris. In this not-so-awful hotel room, with a view almost too painfully perfect to take in. She would go to the top of the Eiffel Tower. Tomorrow.

Benoît had been gone for over an hour.

Lili Gaudet, she could talk.

Marie stepped back into the room. She changed into Ellen's red kimono, but it no longer felt like hers. She got on the bed and stretched out next to Caitlin, stroking her hair, her soft white-blond hair.

"Hi Caty Bean," she said to the sleeping girl.

And then, Benoît Doniel had been gone for two hours.

Marie took her backpack into the bathroom and scrubbed it with hotel soap and dried it with the hotel blow dryer. Caitlin did not wake up. Marie removed all of her belongings from the paper shopping bags and carefully, slowly, repacked her backpack. Making everything fit better than it had before.

Benoît had been gone for three hours and twenty-eight minutes. Even Lili Gaudet could not talk for that long.

Marie got back into the bed and did what she would do in prison, when she was in dire need of comfort. She read *Virginie at Sea*. It was a different book now, knowing what she knew, but Marie started at the end, as she often did. Virginie walked away from the sea lion that she had spent the summer trying to save, knowing that it would die. She walked into the water, still wearing her clothes, until she could no longer stand, and then she dove into the water, swimming out, deeper and deeper, into the dark blue sea.

The ending changed for Marie every time she read it. There was no way to *know*: Would Virginie, left floating on her back in the final sentence, turn around and swim back to shore? Or would she keep swimming, disappear, drown? Could she somehow stay there, forever suspended in time, floating?

Everything had changed, knowing what Nathalie had chosen for herself. There was no hope to be found in *Virginie at Sea*. No solace. No comfort. Nathalie had not lived long enough to publish her beautiful little book. Like Juan José, she had chosen death.

Marie looked at Caitlin on the bed, sleeping. Her tiny heart was beating underneath that red tank top.

What had happened to Juan José? In prison?

Marie went backward in the book, looking for answers. She reread the one sex scene in the novel, where Virginie, a virgin, seduces the reluctant older marine biologist. He knew everything there was to know about sea lions, but Virginie understood that he did not love her, and therefore, she did not love him. But she seduced him anyway. Virginie undressed the marine biologist, piece by piece, taking off her own clothes, placing his shaking hand on her teenage body, daring him to reject her. Virginie was unhappy, and she thought that a profound experience would make her feel less so. It did. The hard thrusts of the marine biologist were painful, almost violent, and Virginie felt strangely awake for the first time. She cut her back on a rock in the sand, bleeding, as she joked after, from two holes.

Marie remembered reading this scene for the first time, thinking about how she had lost her own virginity, drunk out of her mind, to Harry Alford, who had also been drunk, on the hard floor of a stranger's closet. Knowing that Ellen was somewhere downstairs, wondering where her boyfriend was.

Virginie at Sea was no less beautiful, but Marie could not love the book the way she once had. Virginie started out alone and she ended up even more alone. Virginie was dead, as dead as Benoît's dead sister, as dead as Benoît Doniel was to her.

Marie fell asleep with the light on, the book open on her chest. She woke up in the middle of the night, expecting Ellen, expecting the police, thinking she had heard fists pounding at her door, but she had been dreaming. There was only darkness and the sound of Ludivine, meowing, scratching at the door.

Benoît had been gone for five hours and forty-two minutes.

"Marie," Caitlin said, shaking Marie awake. "Marie, Marie, Marie."

The room was still dark. Marie was surprised to see Caitlin dressed in her red tank top. Hadn't they packed her pink nightgown? She had been dreaming about prison, again. They were serving meatloaf in the cafeteria, and Marie, who had never liked the meatloaf, was arranging to trade her dinner for two oatmeal cookies with a woman named Sheila who was in for stealing cars. A guard interrupted them before the transaction could be completed and said that trading food was forbidden. In the dream, Marie had been heartbroken.

Opening her eyes, Marie expected the cement wall of her cell, not the floral wallpaper of the Parisian hotel room. Marie spread her arm onto the other side of the bed. Still empty. Marie looked at the clock. Benoît Doniel had been gone for six hours and thirty-two minutes. The number jumped on the display as she did the math, making it thirty-three minutes.

Caitlin continued to poke Marie. Her hair was dirty, matted against her head.

"Hey you," Marie said.

"Hi Marie."

The door to the balcony was still open.

"I think we're up in time for the sunrise," Marie said. "Should we look? Let's go see."

Marie rubbed her eyes. She put her legs on the floor, she stood on these legs, she was out of bed. She did not want to get out of bed, but she did, because Caitlin was already awake. Benoît had not come back. She picked up Caitlin, taking her to the balcony.

"Look at that," Marie said, boosting Caitlin in her arms. The sun was a great big orange ball, rising above the red rooftops, disappearing between clouds and then reemerging. The washed-out sky was gray, but slowly turning blue. The Eiffel Tower filled the same place in the sky as the night before. Marie held her hand over her eyes to block the sun.

Caitlin imitated her. Marie smiled, pleased by Caitlin's undeniable cuteness. She felt a swelling of love and that caused something to shift, break in her chest, relax. This was the situation, like Juan José showing up at her door, bleeding. What mattered was what you did next.

"Hi Marie," Caitlin said.

"Hi Caitlin."

"Hi Marie."

"Hello Caitlin. Good morning to you. Top of the day. Hello hello. *Buenas días. Bonjour.*"

Benoît really and truly had not come back. He would come back, of course, he would have to, he would return for his daughter, wouldn't he? Maybe he wouldn't. He had spent the night with the French actress. Lili Gaudet. It was such a ridiculous name. She had such stupid hair. Why didn't she get it cut?

It didn't matter.

Unlike Virginie, unlike Nathalie, Marie was not all alone in the world. She did not need Benoît Doniel. She did not want him. Marie was with her favorite person in the world. Her better half. Marie touched the top of Caitlin's head. Caitlin's hair was greasy, but there was no time to wash it. The sun was rising. They needed to move, fast, in case Benoît Doniel was coming for them. It was an odd déjà vu. She had left him only the day before.

"Let's get dressed," Marie said. "Let's get breakfast. What do you want for breakfast? Do you want more strawberry jam? Yes?"

"Yes."

"Do you want strawberry jam and croissants?"

Caitlin nodded her head, smiling.

"Yes. Sants. I want one."

"Do you want to get a little clean first?"

Marie felt competent. She knew how to take care of Caitlin. She did not need Ellen telling her how. Caitlin lifted her arms while Marie took off her tank top. Nor did she struggle when Marie carried her to the bathroom, undressed her and started the shower.

"Let's take a shower. We've never taken a shower together," Marie said, surprised by the false cheer in her voice. "Keep your eyes closed, okay?"

There really was no time for this shower, if Benoît was going to come for them, but Caitlin would get cranky if she was dirty. Once they left the hotel, they might not have another chance for a while. Marie did not know where they were going. So Marie washed herself and she washed Caitlin; she even washed Caitlin's hair, because it was clear Benoît Doniel was not on his way. It was ridiculously early in the morning and he was with his French actress, lying entwined on those perfect flowered sheets. He was a fool. He was an idiot. He was in the wrong place. He had left his daughter alone with a convicted felon.

Marie even washed her own hair.

Marie dressed Caitlin in the clothes from the day before, and Caitlin did not complain. Everything was different, far from their routine, but Caitlin still seemed fine. Or she knew, somehow, not to complain. Marie was grateful. Caitlin drank the warm milk Marie poured into the plastic hotel cup while Marie gathered their things, glad she had taken the time to repack her knapsack the night before.

"Jam and croissants," Marie said, taking Caitlin's hand, opening the door.

Benoît Doniel wasn't there, on the other side, racing to catch them. Ludivine was gone. Marie had forgotten about the cat until she saw the empty ashtray. She did not remind Caitlin. They took the stairs instead of the elevator, in case Benoît was on his way up. It was only two flights. Caitlin held on to the banister and took the stairs one at a time; she was getting better and better at stairs. Marie checked out with a different clerk at the front desk, and in exchange for the room key, she received her passport.

She grasped her hand around the thin blue book. Pressed it against her chest. She had gotten it back.

They were free.

Still free.

Marie remembered walking out of the prison, that thick sense of dread. Her mother had promised to pick her up, but in the end, she had not come. Her lover wasn't getting out, ever, because he was dead. Freedom had seemed a cruel punishment of its own.

Not now.

Look at where she was.

Paris, France.

People dreamed of going to Paris. The air felt good. There were chocolate croissants to eat. Baguettes to carry under your arm. Bowls of coffee to drink. A tower to conquer. A life to begin.

"We're free," Marie said to Caitlin, squeezing her hand. She began to skip, urging Caitlin along the sidewalk.

They had already stepped past the body when Marie saw Ludivine, on the curb, lying flat. The day before, the cat had been sick and needy, a genuine horror, but now she was dead. Marie quickened their pace, relieved that Caitlin had not seen the dead animal, already allowing herself permission to erase the image from her own memory. Marie was in no way responsible for the cat's death. Ludivine had had her shot at Paris and she could not cut it. If this had been Mexico, and if Ludivine had been a chicken, Juan José's family would have cooked her for dinner.

Marie was surprised by how difficult it was to get to the top of the Eiffel Tower. The line was long and Caitlin was cranky. Benoît was supposed to have come back with a nightgown and her stroller. Everything would be better for Marie if she had that stroller. Caitlin would have hummed to herself while waiting in that crazy long line, happy in her stroller, blocked from the sun by the clever stroller overhang. Instead, forced to stand, Caitlin required constant entertainment.

"That is the thing, Caty Bean," Marie told Caitlin, "about dreams."

Caitlin looked at Marie.

"You think you want to do something," Marie said. "Like go to the top of the Eiffel Tower. You think that if you ever go to Paris, that is one thing that you have to do, and then when you get there, boom, you don't want to. The appeal is all gone. You're left with your own taste of bitter disappointment."

Marie had been so sure of Benoît Doniel, and her illusions

of love had dispelled so quickly. It would have been better if she had never met him. Even the name she once loved to repeat like music in her head—Benoît Doniel—was ruined. Marie appreciated the fact that she could say anything to Caitlin, and to some extent, the girl would never understand. Bitter disappointment. She was speaking about Caitlin's father, but maybe she also *did* mean the Eiffel Tower. There it stood, towering above them, so close, but still far. Impossible. They would never last, Caitlin and Marie, they would never even make it to the ticket counter.

Caitlin had started to punch Marie in her legs, something she had never done before.

Marie stared up at the massive structure. It was less impressive when you were standing at its edge; it was almost ugly, just large strips of metal. No bright lights illuminating the sky. Just a tall metal structure, without magic.

"Paris," Marie said, scooping Caitlin up off the ground so she could no longer hit her, and turning around. "Paris sucks."

The only logical thing to do next would be to find something wonderful to eat. A reward. Marie didn't know how to entertain Caitlin in this new and uncertain environment. Marie wished that Caitlin would tell her where to go, what to do. In New York, the little girl had favorite places. In Paris, they were both off balance, confused.

"My fish was named Paris."

Marie nodded. She did not want to talk about the goldfish. Caitlin didn't need to remember the ways in which she had been failed. Instead, Marie bought Caitlin an Eiffel Tower snow globe at a gift stand. She shook it and they watched the artificial snowflakes fall.

"Give me," Caitlin said.

Ellen would have demanded a please. Marie handed it over. Caitlin turned the snow globe over, watching the snowflakes fall on the Eiffel Tower, over and over again.

A well spent three and a half euros.

Marie didn't need to panic about money. She had two and a half thousand euros. She could find a cheaper hotel in a cheaper neighborhood. Marie was thirty years old. Maybe it was time for her to stand on her own. While most people her age had been finding themselves, getting jobs, losing jobs, going to graduate school, getting married, getting divorced, having children, Marie had been to prison.

"Paris Paris Paris," Marie said to Caitlin.

She would have liked the city much more if everybody spoke English. Marie took Caitlin's hand and they began their walk away from the Eiffel Tower. She would not look back. At the first food stand they passed, she bought a ham and egg baguette sandwich.

They sat on a bench in front of a bed of flowers. The city was impressively landscaped, if nothing else. Marie was stunned by the shock of nostalgia, biting into the crunchy bread: the taste of the ham, the thick slice of hardboiled egg, the tomato and mayonnaise. It made her remember a more innocent time, in Ellen's kitchen, when Benoît Doniel had made her this very sandwich. It tasted better in Paris, but something was missing. The delight. The wonder. The pleasure of sitting at the table, watching Benoît slice the bread, wash tomatoes in the sink. The sandwich had cost Marie nine euros. Ellen would come home and sit at the round wooden table in her lovely kitchen, and she would be all alone.

Marie took another bite. It was simple and delicious. Marie did not believe in regret. It could take Benoît Doniel half an hour to make Marie one of these. He had been slow and distracted in the kitchen. Once she got started, Marie could create a never-ending list of faults.

"I don't believe in regret," she told Caitlin.

Their conversations had become one-sided.

It was time to move. Make some progress. But Caitlin was a slow, indifferent walker, easily distracted. Marie recognized the hired help, the black women pushing white babies in expensive strollers, the same phenomenon in Paris as in New York, and Marie followed them. The nannies led her to a children's playground, almost an amusement park really, though no entry fee was required. The place was mobbed with children.

"Horses," Caitlin said.

There were horses. The nannies had led Marie to a carousel, a beautiful old-fashioned carousel, playing music, filled with French children riding all sorts of painted horses. As the carousel went around, these children stood up on their horses, reaching for brass rings that hung from above.

"Do you want to ride it?" Marie asked.

Marie wanted to ride the carousel. She didn't ever remember riding one. Ever. How was that possible? One more thing her mother had denied her. Marie picked up Caitlin once again and walked to what was obviously a ticket counter.

The teenage girl with the purple hair and nose ring looked at her, and Marie realized she did not know how to buy carousel tickets. She was in France. Where they spoke French. "I'd like two tickets," she said.

The girl said something. In French.

"Two tickets."

Marie pointed at herself and Caitlin. She put a five-euro bill on the counter. She faced off with the girl, who took the bill, twirled it in her finger, nodded, and gave Marie two tickets and several smaller coins in return.

"*Gracias,*" Marie said.

She remembered the right word a beat too late. *Merci.* French in France. Spanish in Mexico.

There was another line to ride the carousel. Marie juggled Caitlin in her arms.

"I've got to put you down," she said.

"Up," Caitlin said.

She was tired, reverting to one-word sentences. They had not been out for that long, had not even lasted an hour waiting for the Eiffel Tower, but Caitlin had stopped trying. It was all on Marie. Every single thing. It wasn't fair. She put Caitlin down. Her arms were tired. Caitlin was not a baby.

"Up."

Caitlin started to cry, her face turning red, her wail progressively louder. The black women who led Marie to the park turned to look at her, their faces knowing. Their children were not having tantrums. Caitlin had only had one other significant tantrum of record: when Marie and Benoît first began their flirtation.

Marie picked Caitlin back up.

"Let's just watch for a while," Marie said. "Shh, shh, shh. It's okay. We can ride it later. That will be all right. Come, come. Shh. Please. Please be quiet."

Marie got out of the line, looking for a place to sit down, but all the benches close to the carousel were full.

"Damn," Marie said.

"Damn," Caitlin repeated.

It was idiotic to be mad at a tired two-and-a-half-year-old girl. Marie would not be angry. She wondered if they could sit on the grass, find a good spot where Caitlin could calm down, maybe take a nap. But there were so many people. Marie could not risk Caitlin being trampled. She would have trouble explaining that to Ellen. Marie watched as an old woman stopped not far from them and lifted a little boy from a stroller. Marie eyed the stroller with longing.

"You are so heavy," Marie said to Caitlin. "Caty Cat. I am going to put you down and we'll walk a little. Just a little."

"No."

"No," Marie repeated.

Caitlin pulled on a strand of Marie's hair.

"Stop that," Marie said.

Caitlin let go of Marie's hair. Instead, she started to twist the strap of Marie's tank top around her finger. Marie's favorite person in the entire world was getting on her nerves. She put Caitlin down again, and Caitlin started to scream. Marie thought of Ludivine, and then she remembered that Ludivine was dead, and Marie picked Caitlin back up.

"You are tired, aren't you?"

"I want home," Caitlin said.

Marie returned her gaze to the now empty stroller. The old woman was probably the boy's grandmother, not a nanny. She pushed the stroller beneath a tree directly next to where Caitlin and Marie stood, and then went to the end of the long carousel line. Marie watched as the carousel stopped, and a stream of children got off. The conductor helped the old woman with the steps. Marie watched as the little French boy picked out a horse.

"There we go," Marie said. "A stroller, Caitlin. Just for us. Do you want me to push you for a while? That would be better, wouldn't it?"

Caitlin nodded. She accepted this offer as if she were doing a favor for Marie; for the first time, she reminded Marie of Ellen.

The music on the carousel started. The grandmother sat on the horse, holding the little boy in her lap. Marie and Caitlin examined the stroller.

"This looks nice," Marie said. "Like yours."

"It's red," Caitlin said.

"Your stroller is red, too," Marie said. "Why don't you get in?"

Marie lowered Caitlin and fastened the straps, snapping the buckles, which were not much different from an American stroller. Marie found a baby bag beneath the seat, packed with a clean diaper, a package of butter cookies, a plastic bag filled with miniature French cheeses wrapped in tin foil, and a sippy cup. There was also a blue-and-white-striped sweater that Caitlin would need soon, when it got dark.

"Here," Marie said, and brought the sippy cup around front. Caitlin took it and started to drink.

"Is that good?" Marie asked.

Caitlin didn't answer. She drank whatever was inside. The carousel began turning. The grandmother and child were out of sight, on the other side. Marie started to walk, not too fast, she hoped, but not exactly slowly, either.

It was official. Marie was an indisputable criminal: She'd graduated from the world of petty theft, risen beyond the rank of accessory. Marie imagined the old woman's shock, coming off the ride to discover her stroller gone. It seemed worse, somehow, than taking an actual child. Caitlin and Marie, they belonged together.

Marie had never seen a Marx Brothers film.

They went to see *Duck Soup* in a small movie theater on a side street off the Champs-Élysées, not far from the carousel. The theater was in the basement, dingy, small, empty. Marie drank a beer that she bought inside the theater. The word for beer was almost the same in French. Marie ate the delicious butter cookies she had found in the stroller, and leaned back in her seat, drinking and laughing, while Caitlin napped.

Marie drank a second beer, and then a third.

When they wandered out of the movie theater, it was dark. Marie blinked, thoroughly disoriented. She did not recognize the street they were on, or know where to go next. She knew they were in Paris. The subtitles had been in French.

"I am hungry," Caitlin said, cranky.

Marie was also cranky. She was hungry, too. She wanted to return to Ellen's brownstone, to open the stainless-steel refrigerator and find the perfect thing to eat. On nights when she was this tired, Marie would microwave a bowl of already cooked macaroni and cheese, add extra milk and stir.

"What do you want?" Marie asked Caitlin. "Tell me."

Marie's expectations were low. Caitlin's disorientation in Paris was worse than her own. Marie felt a surge of love when Caitlin provided the obvious answer, McDonald's.

"McDonald's," Marie said, grinning.

There was an answer to every question, as long as she stayed calm.

Marie found a McDonald's on the Champs-Élysées, just around the corner from the movie theater. Marie's hamburger, the Royale Deluxe, came with a strange mustard sauce and was served on a small, good roll instead of an ordinary bun.

Marie liked it very much.

Marie ordered another beer. She wasn't drunk; it was the alcohol that allowed Marie to stay calm. She had every reason to be afraid. She was in Paris at night with a little girl who wasn't hers. But Marie had beer and she thought of Harpo Marx and she was fine.

Caitlin was pleased with her chicken nuggets. They seemed to be no different from American McNuggets. McNuggets like these had also been served at the prison; it had been one of the inmates' favorite dinners. Caitlin and Marie shared an order of french fries.

They were safe.

Benoît Doniel had not found them.

How could he? Paris was an enormous city. Marie didn't have a cell phone. Or a credit card. There was no way Benoît could know where they would go, because Marie had no idea herself. She was taking her time finding a hotel, but she would find one, a hotel with a bathtub. And then, she would go on from there.

Benoît would not call the police on her. Marie was fairly certain of this. He was in too much trouble already, with his wife, with his French actress, with that overbearing neighbor next door. With Marie. He was guilty of his own crimes.

Marie finished her beer.

"Where do you want to go next, Caty Bean?"

"Where is Mommy?" Caitlin said, dipping her McNugget into the dipping sauce like a fast-food pro.

"Work?" Marie said. "Do you miss her?"

It was not a smart question, but Marie asked it. Maybe it was the beer. Maybe it was the situation. Juan José's mother had been overjoyed when Juan José came home. She had embraced Marie as if she were one of her own. But in Paris, there was no warm welcome for them. Instead, they were homeless. It was not supposed to be this way: Marie and Caitlin sitting in a McDonald's, Caitlin's things in the apartment of the French actress, Benoît Doniel in the arms of the French actress. Ellen crossing the ocean, law enforcement on her side. Juan José still dead, forever dead.

"I want to go home," Caitlin said.

Marie nodded.

She had every right to be angry at Caitlin, wanting more than Marie could provide, but Marie also understood. She also wanted to go home, and when she thought about what that was, home, she envisioned her small windowless room in the basement of Ellen's brownstone. The stainless-steel refrigerator full of food, the claw-foot bathtub. Maybe they could go back, Caitlin and Marie. Return without Benoît. Ellen wouldn't need to feel jealous because she would no longer want her husband. Even Ellen deserved better than Benoît Doniel. She had deserved better than Harry Alford. Marie had been jealous of Ellen all her life, but when she actually thought about Ellen's life, when she bothered to think about it, it didn't seem all that great. Her daughter, for instance, had just been kidnapped.

"Your mommy fired me," Marie said.

Marie understood that Caitlin would not understand this. She understood that it was ridiculous to feel self-righteous, given the circumstances, but nevertheless, she did.

"I want Mommy," Caitlin said.

"Not me?" Marie said.

"Mommy."

A bad smell was coming from the spot where Caitlin sat: the undeniable, unavoidable smell of shit.

"Do I need to change your diaper?" Marie said.

Caitlin nodded.

Marie felt resentful. First she had been slighted. Now she would have to change Caitlin's diaper. She would not be paid for changing this diaper. She would not be appreciated for changing this diaper. She had even paid for the diaper herself.

"You smell bad, Caty Bean," Marie said.

There was nothing to do but change Caitlin in the bathroom of the McDonald's.

Caitlin's shit was a runny green.

"Terrific," Marie said.

There was no changing table, so Marie put Caitlin into the sink. Caitlin started to cry, and this time she was inconsolable. "Mommy," she cried.

Marie did not see how she could fix this situation; she felt unspeakably awful, almost helpless, though being helpless was not an option. Marie picked up Caitlin, leaving the dirty diaper in the sink, and rocked her, sang to her in the McDonald's bathroom. With the diaper off, the runny shit had begun to drip down Caitlin's leg, onto Marie's hands, but she did the best she could. Caitlin continued to cry. Marie gave up on her song. She put Caitlin back into the sink and tried to clean her, but was unable to do so, because Caitlin's legs were flailing. Marie was growing more and more frustrated.

"We could be done by now," Marie said.

Two pretty French teenagers came in, whispered something to each other in French, and then left. The paper towels were too scratchy for Caitlin's soft bottom. Caitlin continued to howl.

"Please," Marie said. "Come on, Caitlin. Please. I am almost done. Please."

Marie's voice was taut with barely suppressed rage. She had drunk too many beers. She had not finished her hamburger. She wet a paper towel under the leaking faucet and desperately tried to wipe Caitlin clean. She cleaned Caitlin's hairless vagina, her pudgy thighs, trying to be gentle, trying not to get Caitlin wet. It didn't help that the sink was covered with Caitlin's runny green shit.

A young woman wearing a head scarf and a McDonald's uniform came into the bathroom. She said something to Marie in French. Always French. Maybe she was offering help. Marie needed help. Caitlin continued to cry.

"*S'il vous plait*," Marie said, pointing to the diaper in her hand. Marie kissed Caitlin's head. At least her hair was clean. "You don't have to cry. We're almost done. We're almost done."

Marie lifted Caitlin from the sink and held her midair while the McDonald's employee put the diaper on Caitlin.

"Thank you," Marie said. "*Merci.*"

The woman did not accept Marie's thanks. She looked at Marie with open disgust. She went to the other dripping sink and washed her hands.

Caitlin, at least, was clean. She had stopped crying. Marie held Caitlin to her chest, rocking her, patting her head.

"It's okay, it's okay," Marie said over and over. "It's okay."

Marie had had it with the City of Lights. The fucking Eiffel Tower. Overpriced baguette sandwiches. Benoît Doniel. Marie had done Ellen a favor, revealing his true nature, but that did nothing to help Marie. She would get no reward. This knowledge could not begin to make up for her own bitter disappointment. Marie pushed Caitlin down the Champs-Élysées, stunned by the blare of headlights, the wide road filled with cars, white lights strung over trees, lining a massive structure that Marie recognized as the Arc de Triomphe. This realization brought Marie no pleasure.

"Horsey," Caitlin said.

It was not a carousel horse, but an actual horse, with a policeman sitting astride the large animal. They were coming directly toward them, the horse's hooves jarringly loud on the pavement. Marie did not expect to be caught that quickly. Not now. Not when she had still had so much money in her pocket. Was she that incompetent? With Juan José she had made it all the way to Mexico. They had spent several happy months together. Marie kept on walking, pushing Caitlin's stroller, suddenly determined to make it to the Arc de Triomphe, even though she had absolutely no interest in the monument itself. She would not let the police officer stop her. Marie understood that she would be sent back to jail. Marie was not ready to go back to jail. She had not eaten escargot.

Marie's eyes darted toward the thick row of bushes lining the wide sidewalk. She wondered if she could hide there, but the police officer was already upon them; it was too late. Marie remembered that horrible moment in Mexico, the police officer grabbing her, yanking her arms behind her back, the metal handcuffs tearing into the thin skin of her wrists. She had had no idea handcuffs could be so painful.

The police officer rode right by Marie.

He was gone.

Marie puked into the bushes, and then, without missing a beat, she wiped her mouth with her hand and kept on walking.

"I love you, you know," Marie told Caitlin.

Caitlin did not seem to hear. So Marie stopped walking and knelt down in front of the stroller. Caitlin's eyes were open wide. She was looking at nothing and everything. Marie kissed her cheek. Both cheeks.

"We are so French," Marie said.

She had gotten vomit on Caitlin's clean face. Marie tenderly wiped it off with the sleeve of her T-shirt. She looked at the tall white monument ahead. It was farther away than it had seemed. The Champs-Élysées was not a pleasant street to walk on at night: four lanes of French cars, stuck in traffic, emitting fumes, honking loudly.

Marie blinked, blinded by the headlights.

This was not where she wanted to be.

In prison, when Marie had closed her eyes at night, she imagined the sea, the gentle lapping of waves, stars overhead. She thought of Benoît's book. Benoît's dead sister's book. *Virginie at Sea*. There was beautiful water somewhere in France, a coast to escape to. The Mediterranean.

"Let's go to the sea," Marie said.

Marie hailed a taxi.

"To the train station," she said, confident that her English would work for her. It did.

"Which one?"

Marie did not know. She had no idea. "I don't know. The big one. We want to go to the sea," she said. "The South of France."

"The sea," Caitlin said in a singsong voice.

"You want the TGV," the driver told Marie. "It will get you to Nice by morning. *Le Train à Grande Vitesse*. They go fast. You can sleep on the train. It's good."

"Yes," Marie said. "*Oui*. Thank you."

"Fast," Caitlin said.

"*Merci*," Marie added, grateful.

She hated Benoît Doniel. She did not need to hate the French. The McDonald's employee with the head scarf had helped with Caitlin's diaper. The taxi driver was kind.

Marie fastened Caitlin's seat belt. They had already driven a couple of blocks without it, but that did not matter. Who would Caitlin tell? Caitlin no longer asked for her car seat. Eventually, she would stop asking for Mommy. Marie could do this. They were in the taxi, on their way. She could take care of Caitlin.

She did just as the taxi driver suggested, booking two

tickets on the overnight train. Marie observed the Xeroxed poster taped to the ticket window, showing the photos of two black men. France's Most Wanted. Marie was not on the poster. In France, her only obvious crime was language deficiency.

Marie took the tickets and searched for the right track number. Numbers were not different in Paris, and Marie was able to figure out where to go. She found the track, and then the train, sleek and silver.

"We won't even need a hotel," she told Caitlin.

Marie felt her heart race, could feel the grin spread across her face. She had been ready to give up, but that had been pre-mature. Caitlin was not impressed.

"Where is the cat?" Caitlin asked.

"The cat," Marie said. "Ludivine."

Marie had managed to forget about that sad, wretched animal. The image of dead Ludivine flashed before her eyes, erasing Marie's spontaneous grin. At least, Marie thought, it wasn't the same old request for Mommy.

"She was a bad cat," Marie said. "She had no teeth."

"I have lots of teeth," Caitlin said.

"That is a fact."

Marie had even remembered to brush them. Even in Paris. She might even brush Caitlin's teeth again on the train after they found seats. She would brush her own teeth. They had woken up that morning in a hotel room. Now they were boarding a train. Marie was almost done, had nearly made it through the day.

Boarding the train, Marie was presented with a new set of challenges. Her hands on Caitlin's shoulder, navigating the narrow center aisle, lugging both her backpack and the stroller. The day, in fact, still was not over. They were on the train, but Marie needed to find seats. Everyone was going to Nice, every seat taken. Marie almost expected to see Benoît and the French actress, sitting side by side, reading magazines. Marie and Caitlin walked through one car and into the next and then the next, which became all the more difficult once the train started to move. The train kept accelerating, going insanely fast, too fast. Marie lost her balance, putting her hand on the tops of the seats and sometimes the heads of angry French people.

"*Merde,*" Marie heard, again and again, as she put her hand on top of French people's heads.

"*Merde,*" Caitlin said.

It was not until the last car of the seemingly endless train that Marie found an empty row, facing a young man wearing ripped jeans and aviator sunglasses, reading *Ulysses.*

Caitlin climbed up on her seat to look out the window, pressing her hands against the glass.

"No, baby." Marie shook her head. "You have to sit."

Caitlin looked at Marie, but she did not sit.

"Sit down. Sit down now. Sit down, Caty Bean," Marie said. She longed for the little girl who demanded her car seat. "That's dangerous."

Marie was aware that the man in the ripped jeans wasn't actually reading *Ulysses.* He was watching them from behind his aviator glasses, watching Marie, making her more uncomfortable than she already was. She pretended not to notice him.

"Caitlin, sit. Right this minute."

It was a new tone of voice for Marie. They were no longer friends, Caitlin and Marie. Marie had become the boss; she had channeled the manner of a prison security guard named

Kitty Louise, a dreadful woman who took pleasure in turning the lights out early.

Caitlin sat down. She tilted her head to the side, staring sideways at Marie, the confusion on her face clear. Marie shrugged. If that was how it had to be, Marie could be mean. Now they both knew. She tucked Caitlin under the blue French train blanket she found on the seat.

"Are you tired?" Marie asked.

Marie would give a hundred euros to have Caitlin fall asleep. "Do you want me to read to you? And then you'll go to sleep. Okay?"

There would be no bath. There would be no milk in a bottle. Marie would not take the effort to brush Caitlin's teeth after all. Not tonight. She could not do any more. Marie wasn't sure what time it actually was, but it was bedtime, because Marie was done. Besides those all too brief hours in the darkened movie theater, Marie had not had a moment to herself.

Marie looked directly at the guy in the aviator sunglasses. He had not stopped watching her, which was rude, which was making a hard situation even harder for Marie. There were holes in both knees of his jeans. That could not be a coincidence.

"Do you like that book?" Marie asked him.

Ulysses had nearly given Marie a nervous breakdown in college. She had taken an upper-level English class and the novel had been too hard for her, unreadable, a source of unending torment. Somehow, no one else in her class seemed to share her problem. They were able to turn in papers and speak coherently during class. At the end of the semester, Marie had drop-kicked her copy of *Ulysses* into the campus pond, but that hadn't made her feel better.

"I keep trying to," Marie's seatmate said. He had a low voice, deep. "It's sort of hard, isn't it? But I feel like I am supposed to read it."

Marie smiled, instantly liking him. She had always had a feeling that she wasn't the only person out there who couldn't read *Ulysses*. Her loathing for the book did not, in fact, indicate her own mediocrity. No one in prison cared about James Joyce, either. Ruby Hart used to criticize Marie for wasting her time reading fiction.

The man took off his sunglasses. His eyes were green and bloodshot. He was younger than she'd have expected, in his early twenties. He was unmistakably American.

"Eli," he said, offering his hand.

"Marie."

"Eli Longworth."

With this, he seemed to be waiting for a response.

"Nice to meet you," Marie said.

"Really?"

"Really," Marie said, annoyed. "It's nice to meet you."

"Best supporting actor nomination? The Oscars. Two months ago? You haven't heard of me?"

Marie had never heard of him. Another movie star. His holey jeans did look expensive. He might have been handsome if he did not seem somehow so incredibly ridiculous. The sunglasses, the perfect stubble. Juan José hadn't introduced himself with such arrogance. *I am Juan José, bank robber, love of your life.* He had had some modesty. Marie, however, was all through thinking about Juan José. It was the fault of Benoît Doniel, his complete and utter collapse as Juan José's replacement, that was sending Marie backward, back to a place where she did not want to return.

"Hi Eli," Caitlin said. "Hi. Hi Eli. We are on the train. These are our tickets. Look. Our tickets."

Caitlin had not lost their tickets. Marie wondered if she could ignore Caitlin altogether. The girl was supposed to be asleep. Sleeping.

"What nice tickets," Eli Longworth said.

"Read to me." Caitlin pointed to his book.

The movie star shook his head. "I don't think you'll like it much, either."

But he handed Caitlin his copy of *Ulysses*. She immediately dropped it. Marie picked the book up and handed it back to him.

"There are no pictures," Marie said.

"This book would be better with pictures," the movie star said.

"Read me another book," Caitlin insisted.

All of Caitlin's books were in the apartment of the French actress.

"Hey Caty Bean," Marie said. "What if I sing to you? I'll sing to you and then you'll go to sleep? Okay?"

Caitlin shook her head, no, and then she started to laugh. She was overtired, Marie decided, as usually she was not obnoxious. Or was she?

Because they were in France, Marie sang "Frère Jacques." She sang it three times, knowing that she was being watched. Marie felt herself blushing, singing in front of a movie star she had never heard of. In the fourth round, the movie star started to sing along with her, his voice low and beautiful. By the sixth round, Caitlin had passed out, thumb in her mouth.

"That was sweet," the movie star said. He seemed pleased

with himself. "Your daughter is adorable. You really haven't heard of me?"

Marie shook her head, grinning.

"Sorry," she said.

Eli Longworth named a list of films he had been in. Seven films in four years. Marie had heard of none of them.

"Where have you been?" he said. "Hiding under a rock?"

"Prison."

"No shit?"

"No shit."

"I guess you didn't get to watch many movies in jail?"

Marie shook her head. She had just had this same conversation with another so-called movie star. It occurred to Marie that famous people required people who were not famous to make them feel that way.

"I think some people did," she said. "Not me."

"What did you do?"

"Worked," Marie said. "I worked in the laundry room. Kept my hands clean. I was on good behavior. Trying to get out early to be with her."

Marie nodded at Caitlin. It was easier to feel affection for her again, now that she was asleep. Marie wondered what it would have been like, if someone actually had been waiting for her.

"You missed her?"

"So much it hurt."

"Dude," he said. "That's heavy."

"Did you call me dude?" Marie laughed. "Is that what you kids do today?"

Marie wondered if they were flirting. She thought maybe they were. She was already over Benoît Doniel. Just like that. She would not grieve for him. Not a single second.

"It was heavy, dude," Marie said. She felt like she was a character in a movie. She could be whoever she wanted to be for this movie star. The dried vomit on her shirt sleeve did not matter. The movie star had noticed her breasts. "I did a lot of reflection while I was locked up. Came out a better person."

"A beautiful person."

"Thank you," Marie said, nodding.

"You could be in movies, Marie," he said. "You've got the cheekbones."

Marie could begin to see it, the movie star's appeal, his smooth approach.

"Where's her father?"

"Dead. He killed himself after we were arrested. We'd made a suicide pact, but I couldn't go through with it, not after I found out I was pregnant."

"No shit."

"No shit. We had some bad timing, me and her father."

"Like Romeo and Juliet."

"I guess so."

It was lovely, to think of it like that, Marie and Juan José, star-crossed lovers. Marie put her finger in the hole in the right knee of the movie star's expensive jeans. "You were really nominated for an Oscar?"

"You don't make up shit like that," he said.

"Why not?"

"It's too easy to check."

"In case you're lying."

"You're making me blush, Marie. I'm not lying to you. I can't believe this. You think I'm lying."

Marie smiled, pleased with the way the conversation had turned, that she had a beautiful young man trying to impress her. Benoît Doniel had lied to her about *Virginie at Sea*, but Marie did not see how the young man in front of her could be anything but a movie star.

"I just wrapped a new film," he said. "We shot in Paris, all over the city. It was awesome. Paris is fucking gorgeous, don't you think? I shot my final scene this morning, and I had this amazing brainwave. Why rush home? I'm going to chill on the beach. The French-fucking-Riviera. I have never been there before."

Marie nodded, only half-listening. The French-fucking-Riviera. That was where she was going. It was not a place she had ever thought of visiting before. She also wondered how she could get the movie star to talk more quietly. He would wake up Caitlin.

"Have you heard of Lili Gaudet?" she asked him.

The movie star looked at Marie blankly.

"Who?" he asked.

"An actress," she said. "A French one. She claims to be a movie star, too."

"You're tough," the movie star said. "I haven't heard of her, but I don't know much about French movies. I just met Audrey Tautou. She's a real sweetheart. She's probably the most famous French actress there is. Have you heard of her?"

Marie shook her head, smiling. The movie star smiled back. His teeth were perfect. They were gleaming. He couldn't have been twenty-five. When Marie was twenty-five, she learned how to fold clothes. There was some technique to it. At the end of six years in the laundry, Marie's manual dexterity had increased enormously. If she had worked in an actual place of business, she would have demanded a raise.

Marie looked out the train window. It was black outside, the middle of the night. There was nothing to see.

"I gave birth to Caitlin while I was in prison," Marie said. "I had a friend take care of her until I got out. I didn't want Caitlin to know me like that, you know? A prisoner. I wanted her first memories to be of a happy place."

"That's intense," the movie star said.

Marie had forgotten the movie star's name. She traced a circle with her finger on his knee. An actual movie star. She wished she could confirm this information with someone else. Besides *Duck Soup*, the last movie she had seen was about the vengeful babysitter with the knife. Marie had forgotten about that film. She never got to see how it ended.

"Her hair is so blond," the movie star said, meaning Caitlin.

Marie's hair, of course, was dark.

She would hear this again, she realized, if she did not return Caitlin to her mother. She could dye Caitlin's hair. That, however, seemed wrong. It was not Caitlin's fault that she was so fair. Marie would dye her own hair. She liked the idea, becoming blond.

A new, improved Marie. Maybe in Nice.

"So you are going to the beach?" Marie asked, glad for the fact that her finger was where it was, on the movie star's knee. She moved it an inch or so beneath the fabric, hinting at the possibility of upward movement. The movie star had posed a tricky question, asking about Caitlin's hair, but he didn't seem suspicious. "Is that your plan?"

"Yeah. It is. I'm going to lie on the beach and get drunk. You want to come?"

"Sure," Marie said. "Yes."

"You could hang with me. I'm heading to this supposedly big fucking house my producer loaned to me. I'm not allowed to say whose it is. Because of privacy."

"I want to come."

"Awesome."

The movie star, however, looked slightly confused, now that Marie had accepted his offer so quickly. Maybe she was not supposed to have said yes, but Marie was pleased. She had tomorrow taken care of, and maybe the day after, the day after that.

"Do they sell champagne on these trains?" Marie asked.

Marie's mood had turned celebratory. Caitlin was asleep. The French policeman had not tried to arrest her. She was on her way to a villa in the French Riviera with an Academy Award–nominated movie star. Even Ellen's mother had never thought such glory would be possible. Not for Marie.

"That's a good question. Why don't I check it out?"

Marie smiled.

Caitlin rolled over in her seat.

"She'll need some milk," Marie said. "And maybe a snack, when she wakes up. She likes baguette sandwiches."

"I guess I can do that."

"Because you're a movie star," Marie said.

"You stop that." The movie star shook his finger at Marie.

"Champagne," Marie repeated, watching him go.

He would, of course, pay for everything.

Marie looked at Caitlin, sleeping. With every second, she was getting farther and farther from Paris, from Benoît Doniel, and from Ellen, who was certainly looking for her, carrying a lifetime of barely contained wrath. But Marie was going to the sea, to stay in a villa. Out the window, Marie could see stars, French stars, lighting the sky. She smiled, feeling a gratitude bordering on love when the movie star reentered the train car, returning Marie's smile.

"I got it all," he said.

Six miniature bottles of champagne, three baguette sandwiches, a jug of milk for Caitlin, and three plastic containers of chocolate mousse.

"I didn't know," Marie said, as the movie star poured the contents of a mini champagne bottle into plastic champagne flutes, "that you could get champagne this way."

Life kept on surprising her.

The beach in Nice was not what Marie had imagined it would be. She expected the paradise she had discovered in Mexico: crystal clear blue water, smooth white sand. Here, there was no sand. The coast was rocky; it was all rocks. This was the beach where Virginie had walked out to her own death.

Walking along the rocks was not easy to do. Caitlin fell, not once, but twice, and after that she refused to go farther, sitting down on the rocky beach and putting her thumb in her mouth. The movie star had chosen not to join them for the afternoon. He was getting a haircut in town.

"What if I carry you?" Marie said to Caitlin.

Caitlin agreed.

"I carry you all the time now," Marie said.

Caitlin was starting to remind Marie more and more of her mother, of Ellen. Marie could not hold that against Caitlin, but somehow, she did. They were on the beach, in Nice. It had been Marie's brilliant idea, and she decided to embrace it, being there.

"Look at us," Marie said.

After six years in prison, she was vacationing with the world's rich and famous. Staying in the French Riviera, in a borrowed villa, rooming with a movie star. In the morning, a chef would cook her breakfast. Ruby Hart wouldn't believe it. She had worried about Marie during her final days, had said repeatedly that Marie wasn't ready for the real world. Marie walked into the sea, and dangled Caitlin over the incoming surf, dipping only her bare feet into the cold water.

"It's cold," Caitlin said.

Marie couldn't adjust the water temperature like a bathtub. She hoisted Caitlin way up into the sky and then lowered her down, Caitlin's feet touching the water, again, barely, and then Marie raised her back high.

"Up," Marie said. "Down."

And then up and then down.

"Wild ride," Marie said. "Caitlin going fast. Up and then down and then up and then down and then up. Then down. Then spinning around and around."

Caitlin laughed. Marie could still make her laugh. "This is the biggest bathtub that you have ever been in."

"It's not a bathtub," Caitlin said.

"It's the biggest bathtub," Marie said.

"No," Caitlin said.

"Yes," Marie said.

She spun Caitlin around until Caitlin stopped disagreeing with her. Still, Marie could not get herself to like France. It was not what she thought that it would be. Caitlin was clean, wearing a fresh diaper and the new clothes that the movie star had paid for earlier that day at an expensive children's clothing store on the Promenade des Anglais, but Marie could not quite shake the panicked feeling she had had in Paris, in the bathroom of the McDonald's, her hands covered in runny green shit.

The escargot did not disappoint.

They were served six to a plate at the restaurant inside the Famous Palace Hotel, each snail swimming in a pool of melted butter and garlic.

They had been seated, Marie and Caitlin and her movie star, beneath a chandelier in the center of the dining room. Marie wore the new clothes the movie star had bought her, a black halter top from Chanel, new jeans without holes in the knees, a pair of high-heeled sandals. Marie hadn't felt the specific need for new clothes, but he had made the offer when they were shopping for Caitlin, and Marie accepted.

"Do you want to try one?" Marie asked Eli Longworth, ridiculously pleased with her food. She was surprised by her impulse to share when she knew, instinctively, that she wanted every escargot for herself, and then, even more.

Eli Longworth shook his head.

"I dig France," he said. "But not snails. They are like sea bugs. Gross. But you enjoy."

Marie thought of the French actress. *Dégoûtant*, that was what she had said about Americans eating hot dogs. Lili Gaudet could keep her Benoît Doniel. They could rot together in their shared grief. Marie smiled at her movie star; he did not seem particularly smart. She ate another escargot. She broke off a piece of French bread and dipped it into the sauce.

It was a delicious dinner, one of her very best. Marie had also ordered the lobster bisque and the hanger steak, which was still to come. A tuxedoed waiter regularly refilled her glass of champagne. Marie gazed at the beautiful people in the restaurant. Marie *was* one of the beautiful people. She smiled at a roving photographer who passed by. She ran her hand through Caitlin's white-blond hair.

"I love them," Marie said. "Escargot. I do."

"Order more," the movie star said. "This restaurant is awesome. You look awesome."

Marie wondered, idly, what it would be like, having sex with Eli Longworth, with his long legs and his perfect teeth. Marie also wished she had not ordered an entrée. Her thoughts had drifted, already, to dessert, to the chocolate mousse that would end the meal.

"Hi Caitlin."

"Hi Marie."

"Hi Kit Kat."

"Hi Marie."

"Hi Caty Bean."

"Hi," the movie star said, amused, "hello," but really he had nothing worth contributing to the conversation.

"Soon we are going to have chocolate mousse," Marie told Caitlin. "You love chocolate mousse."

"I love chocolate moose," Caitlin said.

Caitlin clapped her hands. She was grinning, swinging her chubby legs, bouncing them off her thick wooden chair.

This was how it was supposed to be, Caitlin and Marie, happy, pleased with each other, with the food before them, with whatever life offered next.

"You need to try the crème brûlée," the movie star said. He ordered that, too.

Marie did like the crème brûlée, though not nearly as much as the chocolate mousse. She happily ate both desserts, drinking champagne between every bite. It was not much of a sacrifice. Marie returned her fingers to Caitlin's hair, closing her eyes, content.

"We are having fun," Marie said.

This was what tomorrow looked like.

Back at the villa, the movie star did not want to have sex with Marie.

"I am engaged," he told her.

Eli Longworth told Marie the name of the woman he was engaged to. Marie shook her head.

"You haven't heard of her, either?"

Marie had not.

The movie star said that he would be all right with a blow job.

"That's generous of you." Marie was sitting on his bed, watching as he took off his expensive ripped jeans. The villa the producer had loaned him was impressive. It was old, made of stone, had a green lawn in front, a vegetable garden in the back, and a view from the master bedroom of the Mediterranean. Marie looked out the window, at the rolling sea. "But no."

Marie remembered her negotiations with Ellen, when she said that she would not clean or do laundry. She had not expected to have negotiations with the movie star. Even before the escargot, when they were still on the train, Marie had assumed that sex was an unspoken agreement. She was staying in his villa. He was paying for everything, which had seemed only right, considering that he was the movie star and he was also staying there for free.

Truthfully, Marie would have liked to put out; it wasn't the equivalent of vacuuming and making beds. Having sex with a movie star would have felt like an accomplishment. Later in life, she could have told people: *I had sex with Eli Longworth in a villa in France,* and that would have been a good thing, because someone, somewhere, must have heard of him. Marie wanted to have accomplishments she could be proud of, like having finally seen a Marx Brothers movie or eating an escargot. She remembered once, before prison, going to a party and admitting to an older man that she had never seen a Marx Brothers movie. He had looked at her with less interest when he learned this.

"Are you sure you don't want to?" The movie star's voice was plaintive.

Marie was not a prostitute. She did not provide services. She looked at the movie star's knees. Tufts of dark hair grew from a surprisingly skinny leg. He would need to work out, she thought, if he wanted to get truly famous. Marie could no longer touch it, his knee, now that the movie star was no longer wearing pants. Staring at that one specific part of his body, Marie could see nothing attractive about it.

"I find that request insulting," Marie said.

"I get you. I totally do. That was insensitive of me. I sound like a selfish dick. I thought I would have no problem cheating. When I met you on the train, I thought we could have a good

time together, but then I just talked to Jess. She is the sweetest
person, you know. She is an angel."

"I believe you."

"A real angel."

"I believe you," Marie repeated.

Benoît Doniel had loved his wife.

The movie star's fiancée was an angel.

Sometimes Marie felt like she was the only person alive
with any integrity.

The roving photographer at the Famous Palace Hotel, where
Marie had tried her first escargot, was a paparazzo. By
morning, the pictures he had taken were making the rounds
on the Internet. There was speculation that Caitlin was Eli
Longworth's secret love child, that his engagement to the
famous actress Marie had never heard of was over. The movie
star had been alerted to this photo by his publicist in Los An-
geles. Now, he wanted Marie and Caitlin to leave. He had
rescinded his offer.

"Really?" Marie said.

Marie was wearing a pair of black silk pajamas she had
found in the villa. Caitlin was thrilled with her new pink
nightgown, which had purple lace flowers delicately stitched
onto the edges. Marie had woken up hungry, still expecting
a world-class chef to prepare her a fancy breakfast. Marie
wanted an omelet with runny French cheese and sausage.

The movie star had opened a laptop computer on the old-
fashioned wooden kitchen table. Marie leaned over to look.
Marie had not had sex with the movie star, but the outside
world seemed to think otherwise.

"Motherfucker," he said. "I can't believe this. I am in France."

"It's not the best country," Marie agreed.

"Fuck," the movie star said.

"You cursed," Caitlin said. "Mommy says no cursing."

Marie kissed the top of Caitlin's head. She wished that Caitlin would stop thinking about her mother. It would take more than chocolate mousse. Marie stared at the images on the movie star's computer and she knew that she was supposed to be upset. Instead, Marie was fascinated. This was what she looked like. Her hair had gotten long. Her arms were thin, but also strong. This was how Marie looked, out of prison. She looked good. The picture had been taken inside the Famous Palace Hotel. Marie was wearing her new Chanel halter top. Caitlin was on her lap, with her pretty white-blond hair.

Marie did not necessarily like France, but she did like her life; she appreciated life outside of prison. She had had so much fun during dinner at the hotel the night before, eating the expensive food the movie star had bought for her.

"Does Caitlin's nose look sunburned?" Marie said, peering at the laptop. She would not want Ellen to see this photo and become angry.

The movie star shook his head.

"What are you talking about?" he said.

Marie noticed a second photo on the Web site; Eli Longworth was leaning over the table, staring directly into Marie's abundant cleavage.

"My fiancée," Eli said, "is flat-chested."

Marie hadn't worried about the photographer. She had been intent on the meal, one of her best ever. The movie star clicked on to three other Web sites and there were those same two pictures, over and over again.

"You really are famous," Marie said.

"I told you."

Marie helped herself to a cup of coffee. Someone had made a pot, though there was no chef in sight. She found milk in the refrigerator, and she poured some into her coffee and also a cup for Caitlin. It occurred to Marie, staring at the contents of the refrigerator in this borrowed French villa, that Ellen would eventually see these pictures on the Internet and she would know where Marie was. It said so in the caption: *the Famous Palace Hotel.* Marie with her daughter, drinking champagne, laughing. Ellen would come, she'd come to Nice, she'd find the movie star, but she wouldn't find Marie. Because Marie had been asked to leave. Asked politely, but asked nonetheless. The movie star did not seem to mind Marie at the moment, drinking coffee in the kitchen, breathing the same air that he breathed, but soon she would have to go.

But where?

Back home? To her mother's house? That was precisely where she had not gone after prison, the place where she was grudgingly expected, where she was still expected to pay back her debt from the car she had driven to Mexico, a car that had been worth next to nothing. If the police were looking for her, they would have already contacted Marie's mother, told her what she had done. Marie knew whose side her mother would take. Her mother would turn her in to the authorities. Send her back to prison. Marie had no doubt.

Sometimes Marie still could not believe that she had gone to jail. She had run off with her boyfriend; it had been young love. She had done nothing wrong. She had not robbed the bank. She had not shot the security guard. The court-appointed lawyer didn't put up much of a defense for Marie. The white middle-class jury looked at Marie and Juan José with thinly veiled disgust, and she was charged and sentenced, an accessory to murder.

This time, Marie thought, giving Caitlin her milk, this time Marie was guilty. Caitlin was on the wrong side of the ocean.

"You know what?" Marie said to the movie star, not caring what he thought, because a random idea had popped into her head. "I don't have an e-mail address. Actually, I must have one, I had one before I was arrested, but I haven't checked it in forever. Since before prison. I am like an old person. Like that president who did not know about scanners in supermarkets. That is what I am like."

Marie felt a sense of deprivation, looking at the movie star's sleek laptop computer. Her picture was on a page full of celebrities. George Clooney had broken up with his girlfriend, a former cocktail waitress. But it was not just the computer she didn't have, that she was being forced to give up. It was the refrigerator full of food. Real French cheeses and bottles of sparkling water and cured meats and fruits and vegetables. French yogurt. Marie didn't want to leave. She had not had time to take a proper bath.

"You really are going to have to leave," the movie star said. He did not say this gently.

Marie would not be rushed. She drank her coffee. It was good coffee. She had poured her coffee into a bowl. She closed her eyes and she saw Ruby Hart shaking her finger at her. Always giving Marie lectures in the laundry room, that was the part of their friendship Marie had not liked.

"Can't you just call her and explain?" Marie said. "The fiancée? She'll believe you. Because she is an angel. Aren't we having a nice time together?"

Marie was surprised by the urgency of her request.

"Look," Eli Longworth said, but he no longer looked at Marie. "This isn't going to work out."

"I can give you the blow job," Marie said. "If that's what you want."

The movie star sighed.

Marie noticed a beefy-looking man in a suit standing in the doorway. She had not seen him enter the room. His face was stern. It was like a scene from a movie. He had been sent in to deal with her.

"Who is this guy?" Marie said, incredulous.

"Philippe will drive you into town," the movie star said. "When you are ready."

"After I finish breakfast," Marie said.

"Fine," the movie star said.

He no longer liked Marie, which was not a problem in itself, because she no longer liked him. It was unfortunate that she still liked his villa.

Marie got up from the table and returned to the refrigerator. She helped herself to butter and jam, fruit and cheese and a slab of salami. She took a baguette from the counter and broke it in half, and then sliced it down the center, the way Benoît had taught her. She gave Caitlin a piece of this baguette. She allowed Caitlin to put her hands in the jam jar.

Marie returned to the table and proceeded to eat. The movie star and the man in the suit watched Marie, the expressions on their faces deadly serious. Clearly, they regarded Marie as a threat. Marie ate until she was done eating. She did not want to leave, but she also suspected that the man in the suit would forcibly remove her if she did not go on her own. He might call the police.

"I am ready to leave," Marie announced.

As if it were her choice. As if she knew exactly where she would go. As if she was not insanely scared of the situation she was in. Marie had no idea where she would go. She had nowhere to go. Her picture was on the Internet. She could not stay in Nice.

She looked at the movie star.

He drank his coffee and continued to curse at the computer screen, behaving as if Marie was already gone. Marie picked up Caitlin and carried her upstairs to gather their things.

Alone in the master bedroom, Marie found the movie star's wallet in the pockets of his expensive jeans.

"Look, Caty Bean," Marie said to Caitlin, who was jumping on the movie star's unmade bed. "Rich people are careless."

Caitlin continued to jump. Marie hoped she would not fall off. She opened the movie star's wallet. There was no money inside. Marie removed a credit card and put it in the back pocket of her new jeans, but then she returned it. What could she do with his credit card? He was famous. She couldn't possibly use it and get away with it.

Still.

Marie put the credit card back into her pocket after all, a souvenir, and then, on an impulse, reached for a small green glass rabbit that was perched on the windowsill.

Marie moved the rabbit in front of the window pane. The bright light of the day shone onto the glass, spreading streaks of translucent green down the white walls and across the wood floor. Caitlin slid off the bed and tried to chase the beam's light with her hands, smearing red jam on the white wall.

"It's a magic rabbit," Marie said.

"A magic rabbit," Caitlin said.

"The airport," Marie told the driver, surprising herself with how simple it was.

She had to go home. Not back to her mother in the suburbs, but to Mexico, to the place that she belonged. It was so obvious. Marie would return to Juan José's family. To his tiny, dark-haired mother, dressed in black, who would be thrilled to see Marie again, to have a piece of her son's life, returned to her.

Marie spent nearly all of her remaining euros on the plane tickets. Roundtrips were less expensive than one-ways; to go one way was to be considered a potential terrorist and Marie was not that. She had to pay full fare for Caitlin. Before long, she would also have to buy Caitlin new shoes, and replace the books and the toys and the clothes and whatever else it was that Caitlin wanted. That was a worry for another day. In Mexico, Caitlin would play with her Mexican cousins. She would learn to swim in the warm water. She would no longer require things.

Caitlin behaved for Marie in the airport. She sat in her stroller, clutching her glass rabbit, while Marie made her purchase. Her hand shook as she handed over her thick wad of cash, and then her passport and then Caitlin's passport, knowing that the airport could be the place she would be apprehended, arrested. Marie had eluded the police in Paris, but her picture had been plastered all over the Internet. They could be looking for her in Nice. It was the right thing to do, leaving fast. The movie star had done her a favor, pushing her out the door.

Marie's money was accepted. She was given the tickets. She was going to Latin America. Nazi Germans had escaped to the same hemisphere at the end of the Second World War to live long, happy lives.

"I want to hold the tickets," Caitlin said.

"Are you going to be careful?" Marie asked Caitlin. "With the tickets?"

"Yes."

It was not the kind of question Marie had ever asked Caitlin before. She used to rely on Caitlin's judgment completely. Only recently, on the train, Marie had entrusted her with this responsibility and Caitlin had performed ably. The hostility in Caitlin's eyes seemed only fair. She used to be an equal to Marie, would tell Marie when she needed a nap, when she needed to eat, when it was time to go to the park. Now, Marie made all the decisions. The nature of their relationship had changed. They were no longer friends; Caitlin had become Marie's responsibility.

Caitlin snatched the tickets from Marie's hand.

"Be careful, Caty Bean," Marie said.

She would not fight with Caitlin, not there, in the airport.

Marie took the glass rabbit from Caitlin's lap and tucked it between clothes in her backpack. They had only so many nice things left between them.

There was a McDonald's in the airport in Nice. Marie gave Caitlin a choice between McNuggets and a cheeseburger. Caitlin chose the McNuggets. She dipped them in the sugary dipping sauce and they shared an order of fries. They did not go to the bathroom. Caitlin boarded the airplane like an experienced traveler. She took her seat and she buckled her own seat belt.

"I am a big girl," she told Marie.

Staring out the window of the airplane, crossing back over the Atlantic Ocean, Marie let herself remember all of them: Juan José's family, their names and faces coming back in a rush. Uncle Roberto, who had lost a leg in a traffic accident. His older sister, Carmelita, who had three different children from three different men. Maribel, Juan José's favorite niece, the smart one who wanted to go to college in America. His nephews, Tito and Diego and Ernesto. And Juan José's cousins, though Marie had never bothered to learn their names. Marie remembered the chickens, in front of the cement-block house, running behind it, sometimes making their way inside. Marie missed the chickens and the beautiful blue ocean.

Mexico was where she belonged. What she had been searching for, all along. The idea made Marie feel happy. There was a place she would be wanted, loved. She belonged with Juan José's family. She was his widow. They would embrace her, make Caitlin one of their own, just one more child thrown into the mix. They could disappear in Mexico, live out their lives in peace and tranquillity. They would learn Spanish, Marie and Caitlin.

Caitlin would love the chickens.

Marie had forgotten so much.

She had remembered the name of the small town, but she had forgotten about the público, the van from the airport that traveled along the ocean highway, picking up a seemingly never-ending stream of passengers along the road.

Jùan José and Marie, they had arrived in relative luxury, in a car, an air-conditioned car. It was her mother's car, and that had made Marie's mother angrier than anything else, more than the fact that she had run off to Mexico with a bank robber, that she had been arrested. Marie's mother had tried to add the theft of the car to the list of charges against Marie, but the prosecutor had not been willing. She had not visited Marie in jail. Even the parents of murderers visited their children in jail.

"You won't remember this," Marie whispered, smoothing Caitlin's hair, looking out the dirty window at the stray dogs lining the roads, at the children selling oranges and packs of Mexican gum.

From the moment they'd gotten off the plane, Caitlin didn't seem to like Mexico, where strangers touched her blond hair and she was blinded by the bright light of the sun. In the público, crammed between passengers, squashed onto Marie's lap without a car seat or a seat belt, Caitlin wailed, her screams rising above the mariachi music blaring from the radio.

Marie had remembered the beach, only steps away from his mother's cement house, but she had forgotten the poverty. How could she have forgotten? Juan José had robbed a bank to help his family, and all of that money had been confiscated once he was caught. Juan José's family had only gotten poorer since then. His mother's black hair, pulled back into a tight bun, had turned gray. Juan José's older sister, Carmelita, had become old. She was both fat and pregnant.

These two women stared at Marie, standing on their doorstep, carrying a little blond girl. They seemed to take in the backpack and the stroller, Marie's exhaustion. And yet the expressions on their faces were blank. There were no chickens in the yard.

"It's me," Marie said. "Marie."

Marie looked into the cement house. The first thing she noticed was the long crack in the plasma TV mounted on the wall, the same TV Juan José had insisted on buying so many years ago, despite his mother's objections. Marie also recognized the frayed armchairs, the yellow velvet sofa. The woven rug on the floor. A framed photo of Juan José hung on the wall above the couch, a photo Marie had never seen before. Marie walked into the house, past Juan José's small, frowning mother and his large, forbidding sister; she wanted to look at that photo.

She had not imagined him after all. All these years, in

prison, missing him, he had been real. Marie sometimes worried that she had made him up, that their happiness had been a fabrication of her imagination. All that passion. But there she was, standing in his living room. Juan José was grinning at Marie from the wall, so young and so beautiful. He was wearing a dark suit, a white shirt, a bow tie still untied, he was standing on the beach. Barefoot.

Marie remembered that day, that moment on the beach. She had never seen the photo before, but she had taken it; it must have been the day before the police arrived. Marie had been wearing the white dress she would get married in. Following his mother's orders, they had dressed in their wedding clothes to make sure that everything would fit. And then, when Juan José's mother had left them alone for a second, to get more thread, they had snuck out of the house, giddy as children, running to the beach. Because they had wanted to see how they would really fit, together, and they had, of course, fit just fine. They had kissed, wearing their wedding clothes, and maybe that was almost the same as being married. The dress, Marie remembered, was too long, trailing all the way down to the white sand. Marie had forgotten that, too.

She had forgotten that moment on the beach, before Juan José's mother had come after them, furious. She had screamed at them, cursing them in Spanish, and they had ignored her, because they had been happy. Juan José loved his mother, he had robbed a bank for his mother, but he also had never paid her much mind. Marie stared at that beautiful picture, the groom, her groom, and she felt relief but also a fresh wave of sadness, a flood of grief for Juan José. She *was* going to marry him. That had been real. They had been real. The devastation she had felt, waking up day after day, staring at the ceiling from the top bunk of her prison, knowing that she would never see Juan José again.

She had loved him.

He had loved her.

She should have never come back. She should have stayed in France where baguette sandwiches were overpriced, where movie stars were everywhere for the taking. She should be back in jail where it didn't matter what she ate, how she was dressed, what she accomplished. Where every single day was planned, unexceptional and unexamined, sheets and towels, uniforms in industrial-sized hampers waiting to be washed and folded. It would not be so awful to go back. It would not be the very worst thing. If her job in the laundry was waiting for her. If Ruby Hart was still there.

Marie was standing in Juan José's living room and she was crying. It was embarrassing, tears streaming down her cheeks, frozen in front of his photo. Caitlin tugged on Marie's hand, worried.

"Marie?" she said.

Marie picked Caitlin up. There was dirt on Caitlin's face. Her nose was pink from the sun.

She looked from Juan José's mother to Carmelita, searching their faces. She realized, then, that she had entered their house uninvited. It had been Juan José's home. He had brought her here, to this hateful cement-block structure. Marie understood, now, that she was not welcome. She understood.

"You must know who I am?" Marie asked. "Marie? Juan José's *esposa*. I used to live here. With you. You cooked me chicken stew the night I arrived. In celebration."

"*Sí,*" Carmelita said.

The mother spoke to Carmelita in Spanish. They went back and forth, like Lili Gaudet and Benoît Doniel had gone back and forth in French, as if Marie, standing there, waiting, did not matter. If she could have, Marie would have told them that Caitlin was theirs, hers and Juan José's, a piece of him, still alive.

Except that it wasn't true.

And Caitlin had that blond, blond hair.

"Where are all the chickens?" Marie asked, saying something, wanting to prove that she was there, had been there.

"Chickens?" Caitlin said. "I like ducks. And chickens. I like dogs."

"I don't know where the chickens went," Marie said. "They used to be everywhere. In the house, outside of the house. I once stepped on a chicken and it made the loudest noise."

The house, though, was surprisingly quiet. No chickens, no radio, no babies crying. No Uncle Roberto. He was the one who had liked the music.

"Where is Mommy?" Caitlin asked.

Marie felt powerless, unable to stop this, Caitlin's never-ending desire for her mother. She kissed the top of Caitlin's head. Her hair tasted salty, though they hadn't made it to the beach.

Marie noticed Carmelita take in the meaning of Caitlin's question. Marie smiled but Carmelita did not return her smile. Had she hated Marie before? Marie couldn't remember. Everyone had seemed to live and breathe to please her, before, in those months of euphoric bliss. Though Marie was no longer sure. If it had been bliss. She wished she had been in that photo, too, with Juan José, above the faded yellow couch.

"Mommy?" Caitlin repeated.

Marie was starting to believe that Caitlin might actually miss her mother. Maybe, one day, after Caitlin had been safely returned, Marie would tell Ellen that her daughter had missed her. Maybe it was still possible that Marie could get out of this mess that she had created for herself. She could return Caitlin, unharmed, with a slightly pink nose. Ellen would know that her daughter loved her, that her husband was a plagiarist and an adulterer. Marie could be forgiven.

Marie knelt down, to look Caitlin in the eye.

"She went back to the office, Sweet Bean. You know Mommy. She is always working late."

"Where is Daddy?" Caitlin asked.

This question was brand new. Marie decided to ignore it. Marie looked at Carmelita, imploring her with her eyes. The kindness that had come from this family, it would return, as soon as the shock wore off. Until then, Marie and Caitlin remained planted in front of Juan José's photograph, unable to move forward or backward. This was the kind of reception Marie had always gotten from her own mother.

"Can I have some water, Carmelita?" Marie said. "*Agua, por favor?*"

Marie looked at Juan José, who didn't acknowledge her plea for help, because he was just an image, because he was dead. He had done a poor job of looking after her, hadn't he? How had Marie managed to forget that? She had trusted him with nothing less than her life. She had not been unhappy before they met. She might have watched a lot of daytime television, she might have felt a little lost, but Marie had been confident that eventually, when she was ready, she would figure something out. She had believed that.

Now Marie was thirty. Thirty years old and on the run. Again. Her taste in sneakers had not changed. Juan José's family did not love her, did not want her, would not keep her. Marie had remembered that all wrong. She couldn't keep answering Caitlin's questions, day after day after day. But Caitlin couldn't stop asking them. Marie had used the last clean Paris diaper on the airplane.

Carmelita motioned for Marie to follow her, and they went into the kitchen, leaving Juan José in the living room, young and smiling and dead. In the kitchen, Marie recognized the appliances. Flush with bank robbery money, Juan José had bought the refrigerator, the dishwasher, and the microwave. The blender on the counter was in the same place it had been, six years ago.

Carmelita turned on the tap, filling a blue plastic cup with water. Marie refused it.

"Do you have bottled?"

She made the motion of opening a water bottle with her hands. Juan José had warned her not to drink the water. What had been good enough for his family had not been good enough for Marie. Marie had forgotten that, too. Carmelita shook her head.

"*Leche?*" Marie tried. She pointed to Caitlin. "For her? Not for me. For my little girl."

Carmelita opened the refrigerator and took out a box of milk.

"*Gracias*, Carmelita," Marie said.

Caitlin had not entirely recovered from her crying fit on the público. Her eyes were red, her pale white skin mottled. Carmelita poured milk into another plastic cup and gave it to Caitlin.

"Yellow cup," Caitlin said.

Carmelita offered a tight smile to this astute observation.

"You're right," Marie said. "It is a yellow cup."

"At home," Caitlin said. "I have an Elmo cup. And I have a cup with dinosaurs on it. I have a purple straw. My daddy drinks from bowls. Not cups."

Juan José's mother and a teenage girl entered the kitchen. The girl was tall, her black hair long and shiny. She wore a tight T-shirt and was holding a sleeping baby in her arms. It was Maribel, six years older. Marie used to swim with Maribel after the girl had come home from school, after she had finished her chores; they used to go to the store together, after they went swimming, and Marie would buy her candy.

"Maribel!" Marie said, reassured, relieved to have someone at last on her side. Maribel, who she had always liked, who had always liked Marie.

But the cold expression on Maribel's face matched the other women's. She was one of them now. She had joined the other side.

"You remember me? Marie? I was engaged to your uncle Juan José? I bought you candy."

"I know who you are," Maribel said. "You are the *gringa* who convinced my uncle to rob a bank. You are the reason my uncle is dead."

That was what they thought.

That Juan José's death was Marie's fault.

Marie shook her head, but she had no words to defend herself. Marie had not robbed the bank. She hadn't known, when she first met him, a stranger at a bar, that later that same week he would rob a bank. Marie would never have encouraged him. She would have told him that he would get caught. Marie had been caught every time, for everything she had ever done wrong in her life. There was nothing, Marie thought, watching Caitlin drinking her milk, that she could do right. She had loved Juan José. She had loved him and trusted him. She could not be blamed for his death.

And Marie remembered, finally, standing in the kitchen, as Caitlin drank her milk from her yellow plastic cup, that she had always hated being in this house. That Juan José's mother had sewn the wedding dress with an abiding silence, because she hadn't wanted Juan José to sleep in the same room with Marie until they were married, and Juan José had refused to sleep anywhere else. Marie had been fed the best pieces of chicken, and then was resented for having eaten them. The women, they had taught her to make tortillas, a task normally reserved for children. Otherwise, she had been deemed useless, always in the way.

Marie had forgotten all of that.

Caitlin drank her milk standing up, holding her plastic cup carefully.

She looked up and smiled.

"I have a plate," Caitlin said, "with a cow on it."

And then, she continued to drink her milk.

Marie did not know what to do about the silence that filled the room. In the eyes of these women, she had murdered Juan José. They were not going to offer her a bed to sleep in. They were not going to offer her a meal. She could not expect, even, the use of their bathroom.

"Where is Roberto?" Marie asked.

"He's at work," Maribel said. "At the new resort. He washes dishes for white people."

"He has a job," Marie said, hopefully.

Roberto had not had a job six years ago. There had been no jobs.

"He leaves when it is still dark in the morning," Maribel said. "He comes home late at night. His skin burns from the chemicals in the dishwashing detergent. They pay him little. Not nearly enough to support his family."

Marie was disturbed by all the anger directed at her. It had made sense for her to congratulate the family for Roberto's having found a job. She did not run the resort. She did not exploit the local workers. She looked at Caitlin, who had finished her cup of milk.

"All gone," Caitlin said.

No one moved to give Caitlin any more.

"This is all we have," Maribel said. "We need it for our family. For my child."

Marie tried to calculate how old Maribel was. She had been a little girl when Marie left, maybe ten, which would make her sixteen or seventeen, much too young to have a baby. She had been the smart one, the pride and joy of the family.

"That's fine," Marie said, still trying, though it was not fine. It had to be a shock for all of them, Marie showing up like this, without warning. Until the day before, she herself had never considered going back to Mexico. "We have traveled a long way," Marie said.

"Did you bring us anything?" Maribel asked.

"Excuse me?"

"Did you bring us anything?"

Juan José had arrived like he was Santa Claus, the trunk of Marie's mother's car loaded with presents they had picked up along the way. He had robbed a bank, not for himself,

but for them. For this roomful of women. These people, Juan
José's family, they were still struggling.

"Weren't you going to go to school, Maribel?" Marie
asked. "You speak such good English. You can go to college.
Having a baby, that doesn't have to stop you."

"I don't know why you came here," Maribel said. "But we
can't help you. We have our own problems. Go back to your
own family."

Marie blinked.

Caitlin looked down into her empty cup.

"More?" she said.

"There is a resort on the beach," Maribel said. "For people
like you."

"People like me," Marie said. Once Marie had thought she
was one of them, part of the family. "There are no resorts."

"They have built them. You know nothing. They have
taken over our beach. They work Roberto to the bone. Go
and see."

"Where are the chickens?" Marie asked.

"What do you think?" Maribel said. "Where do you think
they are?"

Marie didn't know. She said nothing.

"We ate them."

"All of the chickens?"

There were always more chickens. That was what Marie
remembered most vividly about the house. A cousin could
come home drunk, run down two or three in Marie's mother's
car, they could slaughter a flock for Sunday dinner, and still
there would be more chickens.

"You didn't breed them? Save the eggs? You didn't eat the
last chicken? You wouldn't do that?"

Maribel shook her head. "Times are hard."

The sleeping baby in Maribel's arms had woken up, opening her big dark eyes. The baby that Marie and José didn't have. Marie would have wanted that baby. She would be six years old now.

Marie rested her hand gently on top of Caitlin's head. She closed her eyes, taking a moment's pleasure in that soft hair, just another second, because soon they would be on their way out the door. Homeless once again in a foreign country. More than anything, Marie wanted to keep Caitlin, but she was no longer sure that she could. She had run out of places to run to.

"Hi baby," Caitlin said to the dark-haired infant in Maribel's arms. "Hi."

Marie reached into her back pocket and offered Maribel what little money she had left. The second it passed from her fingers, she wished she had it back.

The beaches in Juan José's hometown had been perfect, pristine except for the trash of the locals, beer cans and skeletons of gutted fish. These beaches had once been magic. Now, making her way along the coast, what Marie saw was a bunch of pickup trucks on the sand and a tall crane, a massive construction site, the metal shell of a building. The water was that same aqua blue, the sand just as fine, white, but the beauty of the place had been ruined. The quiet was gone, replaced by the blare of chainsaws and hammers, the unrelenting beeping of machinery operating in reverse. There were workers poised on iron beams, dripping sweat in the sun, working, making all that noise. Sea gulls fought viciously over a pile of trash on the sand. A Mexican woman was cooking food over a grill constructed out of a metal garbage bin while more workers hovered nearby.

Marie wanted to buy a cold beer. A *cerveza*. The word came back to Marie as she stared at the men. Juan José used to buy the beers, cold and delicious in the hot sun, served with a wedge of lime. They would walk along the sand, drinking, talking. They would wade into the water, holding their beers, as the gentle waves rose and fell.

Marie could not buy herself a beer. She had given Maribel all of her money. She had really done that.

"My ears hurt," Caitlin said, covering them with her hands.

"My ears hurt, too," Marie said.

"Where is Mommy?"

Marie looked at the round curves of Caitlin's small ears. They were a new shade of pink, much like Caitlin's nose, which was also pink. Marie took a T-shirt from her backpack and wrapped it around Caitlin's head.

"No," Caitlin said. "That's a shirt. That doesn't go on my head. No no no."

Caitlin tried to tug the shirt off, but Marie put her hand firmly on top of Caitlin's head and tied a knot with the short sleeves while Caitlin struggled.

The one thing that Marie had not done was yell at Caitlin. She had never done that. Could she tell that to a judge? Could she explain that fact to Ellen? She had never yelled at Caitlin. She had gotten her milk and good things to eat, changed her diapers. She had been good to Caitlin, this entire time. It had been hard, but Marie had tried. She had tried.

"Leave the shirt," Marie said. "Just leave it. Please. You look like a rock star."

"No."

"Please. Please, Caitlin. I don't want you to get burned. Please."

"No."

"Caitlin, please, please leave the shirt on your head. Kit Kat. Caty Bean. For me. Please."

"I want Mommy."

Marie had never hit Caitlin. Not once. That was another thing she had never done.

"I want Mommy." Marie mimicked Caitlin's words. Where was Ellen, anyway? Mommy wasn't there, tying a T-shirt over Caitlin's precious head, doing everything she could. It was Marie, protecting Caitlin from the sun. Worrying about her, night and day. Only now that Marie had become the new Mommy, Caitlin didn't appreciate her anymore. Marie had stopped being fun.

"What if I told you I was your mommy now? What do you think? That I am Mommy? Marie."

"No," Caitlin said.

"Yes," Marie said. "Your mother is never going to leave the office. She isn't."

Marie watched the tears start, watched Caitlin's face twist out of shape as she wailed uncontrollably on a loud and polluted beach in Mexico, a dirty T-shirt tied on top of her head. Marie wasn't Caitlin's mother. She shouldn't have said that. She could never replace Ellen. She had not wanted to. She only wanted to be herself. Marie thought that would be enough.

Marie didn't know what to do. How she could comfort Caitlin? Marie couldn't remember ever wanting her mother. That could not have been Marie's fault. Her mother must not have been a person worth wanting. She must have been the failure. Not Marie.

None of this was Caitlin's fault.

It wasn't her fault that Marie had taken her to Mexico without any sunblock. That Marie had given away all of their money.

And Marie, she wasn't to blame for her own childhood. She had been a child, after all, no more responsible for her circumstances than Caitlin. She had always wanted Ellen's mother, more than her own, but the truth was Ellen's mother had never wanted Marie. She had led her on, introducing her to artichokes and taking her to art museums, writing her clever poems on her birthday, but she never took Marie's side when it counted.

"Oh Caty Bean," Marie said, kneeling in front of the little girl in the sand. "I am sorry."

Caitlin stood there, in front of Marie, and she cried. Her pink face turned red. Streams of thick yellow snot ran down her nose. This was Marie's fault, all her fault. She remembered Ellen lecturing her in the Vietnamese restaurant, telling Marie that she was not to be trusted with her daughter. Ellen couldn't have foreseen the future, this moment on the beach, but she turned out to have been right. Marie was taking deplorable care of her little girl.

"Oh baby, I'm so sorry."

If Marie could have handed Caitlin over to Ellen, right then, she would have done it. Without hesitation. Instead, Marie reached for Caitlin, with the idea of cradling her in her arms. Caitlin pushed her away.

"Not you. Not you. Not you."

Marie stepped back, stunned.

"Not you," Caitlin repeated.

"Not me," Marie said, arms at her sides.

Marie had nothing left. She was out of tricks. All out of ideas. There was nothing left in her backpack. No milk. No chocolate. No fresh diapers. No stuffed animals. No books to read. Nothing. She handed Caitlin the green glass rabbit from the French villa, watched as Caitlin let it slip through her fingers, drop down to the sand. Marie had thought it was a fine rabbit, comparable to the dead sister's silver bangles or Ellen's red silk kimono. Caitlin did not want it.

Marie picked up the glass rabbit and flung it into the ocean. She watched the rabbit land with a splash and then disappear. Caitlin did not stop crying, her tears turning into hiccups.

Marie started to walk.

She started to walk, walking away from Caitlin, who did not want her. Away from the sound of Caitlin's hiccups and incessant wails, away from the piercing noise of the construction crews. She stopped for as long as it took to take off her high-top sneakers, and then she kept going, barefoot on the sand.

Marie walked, not knowing where she was headed. She could walk to the fancy resort she would never be able to pay for. She had no money. She couldn't afford a *cerveza*. But if Uncle Roberto worked in a resort, so could Marie. She could work in the laundry room, live up to her potential, labor side by side with the Mexicans she was so busy oppressing.

How could Maribel think that of Marie?

Benoît, he had blamed her for ruining his life.

The movie star hadn't even wanted to have sex with her.

Everyone thought the worst of Marie. Ellen had never forgiven Marie for Harry Alford. She would never forgive her for this, for taking her husband. Her daughter. Marie had been an idiot to think for a second she could be forgiven. Marie had never wanted forgiveness, not from Ellen. It had been Benoît Doniel who'd betrayed her, who left them alone, in Paris, practically forced them to go on the run. Marie had left prison only a month ago, guardedly optimistic, with no idea

that she would end up back on the same beach where she had
once made love with Juan José. Juan José had killed himself,
hanged himself with a bedsheet, the kind she had laundered.
She had not been reason enough for him to live. Marie had
thought she could keep Caitlin, only she couldn't do it.

"Not you," Caitlin had said. "Not you."

Marie kept walking, leaving Caitlin farther and farther
behind. Step after step. Leaving her entire life behind. Like
Virginie at Sea. Marie could disappear. Become a girl in a
book. It was as if Nathalie Doniel had gotten back inside
Marie's head, providing Marie comfort when she needed it
most. Marie could create her own ending. Like Juan José.
Like Nathalie Doniel. Like Virginie herself. Marie dropped
her backpack on the sand, and began to stride, determined,
into the ocean.

The water never rose past her waist.

Marie walked and walked, but the sea never rose any
higher. Marie looked back toward the shore. The sand was
barely visible, there was only turquoise blue water from every
angle, a flock of sea gulls flying overhead. Marie did not
see how she could drown in this calm, shallow water. Small
yellow-and-blue-striped fish swam in circles around her legs.

"Pretty," Marie said out loud, and then she remembered,
again, what she needed to do.

Marie held her breath and sank down to her knees, and
finally, she was submerged beneath water. Marie closed her
eyes, felt the water flow over and around her, the push and
pull of the gentle waves. She waited. Marie wondered what
would happen next. She felt a fish swim into her leg and then
dart away.

Marie stayed beneath the surface until she couldn't. She

had to breathe. She wanted to breathe. She came up for air. It was all very romantic for Virginie to poetically disappear off the page, but the ending of *Virginie at Sea*, it was complete and utter bullshit. Marie had been deceived. Deceived by Benoît Doniel. Deceived by his dead, suicidal sister. Anybody could write a better book than that.

Marie headed back to shore, swimming feverishly through the shallow water. She had abandoned Caitlin, left her all alone. On a beach. In Mexico. Her favorite person in the world. Of all the wrong choices she had ever made in her life, this was the worst possible thing. Caitlin's small ears exposed to the sun. Her little nose, her pale and delicate scalp. Marie had left her.

Back on the beach, she couldn't see Caitlin anywhere. Marie's backpack lay on the sand in the place she had left it, but Marie didn't deserve to have her things, not the red silk kimono or the Chanel halter top, not the letters from Juan José. Marie left all of her worldly possessions behind and started to run. Marie ran as fast as she had ever run, not knowing how she would be able to live if something had happened to Caitlin. Marie ran faster still, ignoring the piercing cramp in her side, running through it. She had left Caitlin all alone to die, and she would have to live with that knowledge for the rest of her life, not in a watery, poetic blur, but behind bars, this time for murder, first-degree murder, knowing what she had done to her Caty Bean.

And then Marie saw Caitlin, exactly where she had left her. Caitlin had managed to take the T-shirt off her head and was burying it beneath the sand.

Caitlin looked at Marie and she smiled.

"Hi Marie," she said.

Marie bent over, hands on her thighs, catching her breath, taking a moment until she was able to speak. "Hi Caitlin."

"Hi Marie."

"Hi Caty Cat."

"You are all wet," Caitlin said.

Marie gazed at Caitlin in disbelief. Caitlin, playing in the sand as if nothing had happened. Not burned to a crisp. Not raped and murdered. Not kidnapped. Playing. Happy. Marie collapsed onto the sand, putting her arms around Caitlin, kissing her all over. Her blond head, her chubby arms, her shoulders, her beautiful face. Marie made loud smacking noises, kissing Caitlin and then kissing her some more.

"Stop," Caitlin said, but she was laughing.

"I'm sorry I put a T-shirt on your head," Marie said.

"It's all gone," Caitlin said.

She pointed to the small mound of sand on top of Marie's T-shirt.

"You are so smart," Marie said.

Marie picked up a handful of sand and watched it fall through her fingers, landing on top of Caitlin's pile. She scooped up another handful, and began in earnest, building a sand castle.

"Look at our beautiful castle," Marie said. "It's getting tall, isn't it? Do you think it's tall?"

"Tall," Caitlin said. "Very tall."

Caitlin smashed the sand castle with her fists and started to laugh. Marie loved that laugh.

"You don't hate me?" Marie said.

Caitlin looked at Marie.

"Silly Marie," she said.

The sun was beginning to set. Marie's ankle had begun to throb. Sand was encrusted inside of her jeans. Her face was sunburned. She made slow progress, Caitlin heavy in her arms, fast asleep. Marie had walked more than she had ever walked before, swam farther, run harder, and felt more afraid than she had ever imagined possible.

Marie was convinced that Maribel had lied about the resort when she came upon what seemed like a mirage: a high-rise hotel. Sleek and new. There were teakwood lounge chairs on the white sand, hammocks hanging between picture-perfect palm trees, a tiled swimming pool filled with water bluer than the ocean. There was a shirtless Mexican, cutting open coconuts for guests with a machete. Marie shifted Caitlin in her arms, took a coconut, and kept on walking.

"White people's paradise," she whispered to the sleeping girl, before sipping the cool coconut milk.

The receptionist was a pretty Mexican woman wearing wire-rimmed glasses and a blue blazer. She might have blinked when she saw Marie, barefoot and sunburned, carrying a sleeping child beneath a silk kimono, but Marie also might have imagined it. Like Maribel had said, this was where Marie belonged. She felt victorious, reaching this front desk, like a survivor of a long and arduous war who has reached safety at long last.

This was the end of the road.

"Welcome," the receptionist said, "to Las Alamandas."

"Thank you," Marie said, pleased to be addressed in English. "I am happy to be here."

Marie took a deep breath, taking her time. It did not matter how she looked. She was a white person in Mexico. She had a credit card.

"I think I'll take a room, please."

Marie did not ask the price. She did not offer to wash dishes. She rested first Caitlin and then the coconut on top of the hotel counter. She looked at the receptionist and smiled, as if nothing about the situation was unusual. From the back pocket of her wet Chanel jeans, she carefully removed the movie star's platinum credit card and her own soggy passport. Benoît Doniel, she knew, had used Ellen's credit card to buy the plane tickets, leading Ellen straight to Paris.

"A suite," Marie said. "With a view of the ocean."

"Of course." The polite receptionist was impeccably trained. She accepted Marie's offering without any noticeable disdain. She studied the credit card a moment too long. Marie watched her trying to feign disinterest; she gently nudged Caitlin farther onto the counter, making sure she would not fall.

"Oh. Eli Longworth. I loved his last movie. He got robbed of the Oscar, don't you think? Is he here?"

Marie smiled to herself. He had been an actual movie star, known by receptionists in Mexican resort hotels. Marie had refused to give him a blow job. This was the kind of thing Marie would hold on to.

"He'll be joining us soon," Marie said. "When he's done with his shoot."

"Well." The receptionist smoothed her smooth hair. She pushed her glasses back up the bridge of her nose. "That's wonderful news. I am an enormous fan."

Marie gave the polite receptionist all of the requested information: her name, the address of Ellen's brownstone in New York. She watched as the woman ran the movie star's credit card number through the machine, watched as it went through. It did go through.

"Excellent. We have a wonderful room for you and your daughter."

"My daughter," Marie repeated, noticing the ease with which these words flowed from her lips. "She's all tuckered out."

She scooped Caitlin, cradled in silk, off the counter and back into her arms. Marie was surprised when her arms began to shake. She had carried Caitlin so far, miles and miles down a sandy beach. There was not much farther to go. She followed the porter to an elevator. As she had no luggage, he offered instead to carry Caitlin, but Marie refused.

"Mine," she said.

Caitlin wouldn't be hers for much longer. Ellen was winning. Again. Always. She would get her daughter back, and Caitlin would forget Marie, would never know that this had happened. Caitlin would never remember being hungry or thirsty, abandoned on a beach in Mexico.

The porter opened the door and Marie found herself in a spacious suite, high off the ground. Lush, luxurious surroundings. The walls were painted a pale orange, the gauze curtains a pale shade of yellow, billowing gently from an ocean breeze.

In the bedroom, Marie found a king-sized bed, a bouquet of white hydrangeas on the bedside table. It was, without doubt, the nicest room Marie had ever stayed in. She would add this to her list of accomplishments.

"Look at us," she said to Caitlin, kissing the top of her sleepy head.

"Marie?" Caitlin said.

"Hi you."

"Hi Marie."

"Hi Kit Kat."

"Hi Marie."

"Hi Caty Bean."

Marie juggled the girl in her arms. She was heavy, but Marie was loath to put her down. Instead, she licked Caitlin's cheek.

"You taste salty," she said.

In the book she would write, Marie would stay there with Caitlin, forever and always, in this expensive resort hotel. Swim in the tiled pool. Drink *café con leche*s and eat fresh fruit, watch educational Mexican shows on the enormous hotel TV.

Marie opened the doors to their terrace. They had a stunning view of the ocean.

"Look at this," Marie said.

The view was better than the Eiffel Tower. The view took Marie's breath away. There were no pickup trucks, no piles of trash. Only the white sand, the blue water. Rays of pink and purple streaked the sky. Marie could see both the sun and the moon. She kissed the top of Caitlin's head. That soft white-blond hair.

"Down," Caitlin said.

At last, numb with exhaustion, Marie put Caitlin down. Her arms, muscular and strong from prison, were empty.

Caitlin pointed to the sky.

"Orange," she said.

"Orange," Marie agreed. She knelt down next to Caitlin and again kissed the top of her head. She couldn't seem to stop herself. Caitlin did not object. "I see orange. And blue. And purple. And I can see the moon. Do you see the moon? Over there? Do you see it?"

"I do," Caitlin said. "Good night moon."

Marie, she was not going to cry.

"Come here," she said.

She took Caitlin's hand, leading her to the bathroom. Marie could not have been more pleased with what she saw.

"Look at that bathtub," Marie said, squeezing Caitlin's small hand, holding it tight.

It was a beautiful white ceramic tub, wide and deep, with a border of dark blue tiles, like the swimming pool outside. They were both dirty, and while Marie still had the chance, she would make sure that Caitlin was nice and clean. Tomorrow, if there was still time, they would swim in that pool.

"I want to take a bath," Caitlin said.

"So do I."

Marie smiled, envisioning the bath they would take. But

first, she called for room service. Macaroni and cheese, a bottle of whiskey. Milk for Caitlin. Chocolate pudding.

"I like pudding," Caitlin said.

Marie ran the water for their bath.

ACKNOWLEDGMENTS

Bad Marie is the second novel I was afraid would not get written. I'm grateful to my agent, Alex Glass, for believing in it and to my editor, Kate Nintzel, for working so hard on it. Thanks to the Writers Room in NYC, the Edward Albee Foundation, Ann and Ira Dermansky, and Lesley and Harvey Weinberg for providing writing spaces at crucial junctures. Also thanks to my now four-year-old niece, Emma Dermansky, for dialogue tips, and to Lauren Cerand for her savvy advice; to Heather Paxson, Melissa Johnson, Joelle Yudin, Sarah Bardin, Jessica Pallington West, and Robbi Pounds for reading *Bad Marie* in various draft forms; and to Jürgen Fauth for reading every single one.

P.S.

Insights,
Interviews
& More ...

Meet Marcy Dermansky

Jürgen Fauth

MARCY DERMANSKY *is the author of the critically acclaimed novel* Twins *and a film critic for About.com. Her short stories have been published in numerous literary journals, including* McSweeney's, Alaska Quarterly Review, Mississippi Review, *and* Indiana Review. *A former MacDowell fellow, Marcy is the winner of the Smallmouth Press Andre Dubus Novella Award and* Story *magazine's Carson McCullers short story prize. She lives in Astoria, New York, with her husband, writer Jürgen Fauth, and her daughter, Nina.*

About Me

After my first novel *Twins* was published, I was frequently asked: Are you are a twin? I am not. I wonder now, with the release of *Bad Marie*, if people will ask me if I am a kidnapper. And no, I am not.

I do have a baby now, a daughter named Nina, who did not exist when I wrote *Bad Marie*. Clearly I must have had baby on the brain. Now that I am a mother, I wonder if would write the same book. It's impossible to say. For the record, I do have many things in common in Marie.

I love to take baths. I enjoy my whiskey and chocolate pudding. I am always thinking about my next meal and angling for a way to get myself to the beach. Any beach. I compulsively read and read my favorite books, much like Marie reads *Virginie at Sea*.

I have only ever wanted to be a writer. I feel pretty grateful that that is what I am. I have moments though, swimming in other people's swimming pools, when I wonder why I did not become a doctor or a lawyer or a corporate raider. Fortunately, this feeling usually passes. I can take delight in the good fortune of others and rejoice that their good fortune is shared with me. I like to believe that I give back, too, with the stories that I tell, creating books that will be read, again and again and again. ∾

About the book

BAD MARIE BEGAN with the image of a bathtub and a glass of whiskey. I put a naked Marie in the tub, added a baby and some rubber ducks, threw French author Benoît Doinel and his undeserving American wife into the already crowded room. The story took off from there.

I am a novelist, but I also moonlight as a film critic. I probably see more movies each year than I read books. I think it's fair to say that *Bad Marie* is my attempt at writing a French movie. Because of all movies, I love French movies best. One of the biggest treats for me each year is the "Rendez-Vous with French Film" series at Lincoln Center. I get to indulge in French movies, sometimes two or three a day, and in between films, I take myself out for lunch. I experience occasional fits of guilt for spending my time this way, the rest of the world seemingly hard at work, but, as I remind myself, I find genuine inspiration.

I am in love with that moment in François Truffaut's *Stolen Kisses* when Antoine Doinel stares at himself in the mirror and repeats his name. Antoine Doinel. Antoine Doinel. Antoine Doinel, Antoine Doinel, Antoine Doinel. Jean-Pierre Léaud is so good in the role—funny and gorgeous and wonderfully intense. It pleased me enormously when that scene snuck into *Bad Marie*. Marie is in the early throes of love when she stares into the mirror and repeats the object of her affection's name. Benoît Doinel. Benoît Doinel. Benoît Doinel. Just saying it makes Marie happy. Writing those lines, I was happy.

When I close my eyes and picture Benoît Doinel, I see the French actor Mathieu Amalric, who first charmed me in Arnaud Desplechin's *Kings and Queen*, swoopy hair in his eyes, having a fine time in a mental institution while avoiding his ex-wife and the tax collector. If Amalric is in a film, I will see it. I am also in love with French actresses: Isild le Besco, Emmanuelle Devos, Ludivine Sagnier, the incomparable Catherine Deneuve. And yes, of course, that poor miserable cat in *Bad Marie* is named after Ludivine Sagnier, though they are nothing alike. Sagnier is a luminous creature. My fictional cat is missing her front teeth and is covered in scabs.

It both surprised and distressed me when I realized that Marie would have to go to France. I have only spent one long weekend in Paris. I wasn't sure I could pull it off. In fact, I tried to convince Marie to go elsewhere. In an early draft of *Bad Marie*, she and Benoît get into a green Jaguar and ▶

drive to Vermont. They look at the foliage and eat sharp white cheddar cheese. It was wrong, all wrong. Paris was where they had to go, and scared as I was, Paris is where I took them. Out to dinner and down the Champs-Élysées, to the Eiffel Tower and a housing project on the outskirts of town. It turns out, through the movies, Paris is a city I know well. ∾

Five French Films from Which I Have Found Inspiration

1. Guillaume Canet's *Tell No One* (2006)
2. Arnaud Desplechin's *Kings and Queen* (2004)
3. Benoît Jacquot's *À Tout de Suite* (2004)
4. Agnès Jaoui's *Look At Me* (2004)
5. François Truffaut's *Stolen Kisses* (1968)

Five Novels I Have Compulsively Read and Reread

1. F. Scott Fitzgerald's *Tender Is the Night* (1934)
2. Josephine Humprey's *Rich in Love* (1987)
3. Mona Simpson's *Anywhere but Here* (1992)
4. Antonia White's *Beyond the Glass* (1954)
5. Joy Williams's *Breaking and Entering* (1988)

An Excerpt from Marcy Dermansky's Debut Novel, *Twins*

MARCY DERMANSKY'S DEBUT NOVEL, Twins, *was named a* New York Times Book Review *Editor's Choice and was called a "brainy, emotionally sophisticated bildungsroman-for-two"* (New York Times Book Review*); a "witty and slyly subversive take on the teenage American dream"* (Daily Mail on Sunday*); and "compelling, dark, and like a traffic accident that you try to look away from, only to find your gaze returning with odd fascination"* (Denver Rocky Mountain News*).*

SUE

I wanted tattoos for our thirteenth birthday. Chloe didn't. Chloe refused. I told her I did not know what I would do if she kept saying no.

"Tattoos are dirty," Chloe said.

Chloe was four minutes older. She was an eighth of an inch taller. She was smarter. She was prettier. We were identical twins, but Chloe had turned out better. She was the better twin, she had the better name, and I was desperate to hold on to her. Horrifying girls like Lisa Markman were inviting Chloe to their parties and offering her cigarettes and beer and birth control.

My childhood had passed in a ▶

golden bubble of happiness. I adored
Chloe and Chloe adored me. We
didn't need our parents; we didn't
need our brother or friends or parties
or separate bedrooms. Chloe and Sue.
Our hair was blond, our eyes were
blue. For twelve perfect years, Chloe
and I lived and breathed each other.
We took baths in the same bathtub,
shared the same rubber bath toys.
Now Chloe took constant showers,
all by herself.

We needed tattoos.

"I won't," Chloe said. "You can't
make me. No one in the eighth grade
has a tattoo."

She was right. No one did. We
were from the suburbs, I hated every
single person in the eighth grade.
They were all morons, out to steal
my sister. Chloe was much too good.
She was too eager to please.

I sat on my bed, staring at Chloe,
waiting for her to crack. Chloe
wanted her own room, but there
were no extra rooms in the house.
It was a stupid idea. We were meant
to share a room. We were identical
twins. We had no secrets. Chloe
picked up a hairbrush and started
brushing her hair. She was obsessed
with being clean. Chloe was always
taking showers, smoothing her
hair, washing her face, washing

her hands, looking at herself in the mirror.

"You want to be like everybody else," I said. "But they're all boring."

"Who is boring?"

"Everyone."

"Everyone?" Chloe said.

I reached for her hand. Chloe laid down her hairbrush on the bed and squeezed my fingers.

"There is no one like us," I told her.

"Everyone is boring?" Chloe repeated.

I picked up Chloe's brush and threw it against the wall.

Chloe bit her lip, looking down at her hands.

"Our tattoos won't be dirty," I said.

I'd explained it to her. I had found someone who didn't care that we were underage. I had paid in advance. Everything was planned. Our tattoos would be simple. Chloe would get a SUE tattoo. Mine would say CHLOE. If Chloe ever got lost or made friends with someone who was not me or had sex with some strange, awful man, she could never forget who we were. Who we belonged with. It wasn't enough that we looked the same. Chloe could put a rhinestone barrette in her hair and she became someone else. She would get upset with me when I put a barrette in my hair too. ▸

Chloe looked at her brush. It had
left a dark mark on the pale pink wall.

"I can't get a tattoo," she said.

"You have to," I said.

Chloe shook her head.

"We could get our ears double-
pierced," she whispered.

"No," I said. "Tattoos. It's all
planned. It's already paid for."

Chloe crossed the room, picked
up her brush, and started brushing
her hair again. She was so beautiful.
Wherever we went, people stared at
Chloe, they stared at us. I knew that
I looked like her. Technically I was
beautiful too. But when I wasn't next
to Chloe, I didn't feel right. I tripped
on my shoelaces. My hair tangled
easily.

"Three letters," I said. "To make
sure we are never apart. No matter
where we go. You won't do that
for me?"

"It's enough to be twins," Chloe
said. "It's practically tattooed on our
faces. We look the same. Why isn't
that enough?"

We had been having the same
conversation for days. Chloe wanted
friends, boyfriends. She wanted to
blink her eyes and imagine me gone.
I sat down on the floor and cried. I
cried until my chest hurt and then
I coughed. Snot dripped down my

face and my head started to ache.
Chloe sat down next to me and put
her hand on her own head, like it hurt
her too. For a while, she did nothing,
just watched me cry. I'd blink through
my tears, wipe the snot on to my
sleeve, and watch her, watching me.

"Sue," she said. "Why do you do
this?"

And then Chloe wrapped her arms
around me. She rocked me like I was
her little baby. I was miserable, but
I felt wonderful, rocking. We rocked
back and forth. Chloe and I were
miserable together. It was the middle
of the night. I could hear our older
brother, Daniel, in his room down the
hall, strumming chords on his guitar.

"We are underage," Chloe
whispered. She kissed the top of
my head. Our age didn't matter. The
appointments were made. The tattoo
guy had taken my money and told me
how to come in the back door. I had
been slipping twenty-dollar bills from
my father's wallet for months.

One day, Chloe would be glad.
One day we would be old, we would
be thirty, and Chloe would thank me.

Chloe's interest in other girls was
temporary. It was adolescence. The
tattoos, I knew, would keep us safe.

"We could get a computer," Chloe
said. "Or leather boots." ▶

An Excerpt from Marcy Dermansky's
Debut Novel, *Twins* (continued)

"No," I said.

I stretched across Chloe's lap and reached over to open her schoolbag. I took out her pencil case and removed a freshly sharpened pencil. Chloe liked her pencils sharp. She loved multiple-choice tests, filling in the small circles with all the right answers.

"What are you doing?" she said.

I stuck the sharp tip of the pencil into my arm. A bubble of blood spurted from the spot. It was more brown than red. I touched the blood with my finger, smearing it over my skin.

"Why do you have to be so dramatic?" Chloe said.

If I was lucky, the lead from the pencil would make it into my bloodstream and I'd die an early death.

"Stop crying," Chloe said. "You make my head hurt."

I wanted to die. Chloe was the better twin and I was not necessary. She did not need me and soon, any day now, she would pretend she did not know me.

"You should clean up your arm," Chloe said. "You're bleeding."

I shook my head. I hoped the lead would spread quickly. I closed my eyes. If I was dead, Chloe would no longer be an identical twin. She could cut the pictures in half, and no one would know I had ever been born.

She got up. I could hear her walk into the bathroom, hear the water running from the sink. She was washing her face, scrubbing her hands. That's what Chloe did. But then she came back to the room with tissues, a Band-Aid, antibiotic cream. She wiped the tears from my face. She put the cream on my cut. Chloe was a good nurse, but she wouldn't become a nurse. She'd be a doctor, a neurosurgeon. I prayed that she would not want to be a lawyer, like our parents. Our parents were miserable shits. Our parents were raging bores. They were divorce lawyers.

"Stop crying," Chloe said. "Please. Please stop crying."

I would not stop crying.

"Are they safe?" Chloe said. "Tattoos? Are they hygienic?"

I nodded, still crying. I was winning. I knew I had won. "Yes," I said. "Yes."

Chloe bit her lip.

"Everything is sterilized?" she said. "Clean?"

"Of course," I said. "One hundred percent clean."

I didn't know. I had no idea. For ▶

all I knew, we would get hepatitis B and die. That would be fine. We would die together.

"I want mine to be pink," Chloe said.

"Fine," I said. "Pink."

I hated the color pink. The walls of our bedroom were pink. Most of Chloe's clothes were pink. Most of mine were too. I didn't care. I reached for Chloe's hand. I squeezed it tight.

She looked sad. She shook her hand out of my grip, but I couldn't stop grinning.

"You are such a drama queen," Chloe said. ◷

Don't miss the next book by your favorite author. Sign up now for AuthorTracker by visiting www.AuthorTracker.com.